'Flint!' Marcus passed low, a touch of curve.

Flint had outrun his weary teammates. No time to wait for backup. Praying that luck and the skills would stay with him, he cut right with the ball, drawing opposition players away from the goal.

They came for him.

H slowed, feigning indecision. 'Come on!' he ta nted, tempting them out further. 'Come and get it

T o players took the bait.

H surged again, chipping over their heads, blaz-in between them and chasing it. He controlled the ba l, twisted to give a third man the slip, then, arriving in front of the goal . . . *blasted* it.

Also available by Neil Arksey and
published in Corgi Yearling:

BROOKSIE

SUDDEN DEATH

FLINT

NEIL ARKSEY

CORGI YEARLING BOOKS

For my family,
friends and readers

FLINT
A CORGI YEARLING BOOK : 0 440 864208

First publication in Great Britain

PRINTING HISTORY
Corgi Yearling edition published 2000

3 5 7 9 10 8 6 4 2

Copyright © Neil Arksey, 2000

The right of Neil Arksey to be identified as the author of this work
has been asserted in accordance with the Copyright, Designs and
Patents Act 1988

Set in 12/15pt New Century Schoolbook by
Phoenix Typesetting, Ilkley, West Yorkshire

Corgi Yearling Books are published by Transworld Publishers,
61–63 Uxbridge Road, London W5 5SA,
a division of The Random House Group Ltd,

in Australia by Random House Australia (Pty) Ltd,
20 Alfred Street, Milsons Point, NSW 2061, Australia,
in New Zealand by Random House New Zealand Ltd,
18 Poland Road, Glenfield, Auckland 10, New Zealand,
and in South Africa by Random House (Pty) Ltd,
Endulini, 5a Jubilee Road, Parktown 2193, South Africa.

Printed and bound in Great Britain by Clays Ltd, St Ives PLC

'I'll be no more than ten minutes.'

Flint fingered the ball in his pocket. How many times had he heard that before?

The muscles in Dad's hands and forearms corded. The biceps bulged. He hefted the huge, twisted knot of cable up onto the side panel. The pickup's suspension creaked. 'This stuff's worth a bit.' He let the red and black bundle drop back with a bang. 'Stay by the pickup.'

''Course, Dad.' Flint sighed.

'I mean it.' Dad scowled. 'Keep your eyes on it.'

Thick black hair, scruffy jacket and oil-stained trousers. The giant he called 'Dad' rocked his crippled way down the street.

Throwing a final warning glare, he turned and disappeared inside the betting shop.

Taking out his ball, Flint jogged across the road.

The pavement was wide, the wall plenty high enough. And beneath all the graffiti the remnants of a wobbly painted goal were still visible. Perfect.

Flint tossed the ball up into the air. It was only a tennis ball, and a battered, tatty one at that, but – no matter, good enough for keeping the rust off old skills.

It wasn't as if he had a choice. It wasn't as if he could sneak a *football* around in his pockets. On the off-chance.

He booted the ball against the bricks. It leapt back at a peculiar angle. The wall was rougher than it looked. He had to lunge, catching the ball a smart, satisfying crack with his instep.

This time it came back straight. Flint stopped it with his chest. Letting it drop, he twisted, caught it between his heels and jumped, flicking it over his head.

The ball hung invitingly in the air.

Taking a small step backwards, Flint dropped his hips. His legs were compressed springs.

The ball fell.

He leapt to meet it – not head first, but flipping back . . . reaching up with his foot . . .

. . . *upside down* . . .

. . . somersaulting . . .

'*Ba-daah!*' He landed – the right way up, on two feet. Just about.

OK, he staggered a little and nearly lost it, but . . . essentially it was all there. A *bicycle* kick. No mean feat over turf, but over concrete, with a bald tennis ball! You had to be mental. Desperate. Or both. Only regular practice over turf would smooth out the wobbles and wrinkles. Fat chance there was of that.

He moved in closer to the wall, shortening reaction times. Left foot, right foot, left ankle, right ankle, left thigh, right – a player needed to develop control with all parts of the leg.

The ball glanced off the lamppost. Checking for traffic, Flint ran out into the road. 'Past his marker . . . putting on a spurt . . . passing one, two, three of the opposition . . . he *slams* on the brakes, doubles back, wrong-footing another. This boy can turn on a pinhead!

'He looks round – there's no-one to pass to. He'll have to go it alone. *Wow! – look at*

7

that for acceleration! He whips round the midfield . . . weaves, this way then that, through the defence. *And still he keeps going!* Only the keeper now between him and the goal. He cuts in . . . he shoots . . . *he scores!'*

'Give me that.'

'Dad!' Flint span round. 'You're back!'

'You noticed.' The voice was hard with fury. *'Give.'*

Dad had lost. Probably every penny in his pockets.

Flint tossed the ball.

Dad twisted, stretched back his arm and, in one sharp movement, hurled the ball high into the air, up over the roofs of the houses. *'Agh!'* He winced, straightened, put a hand to his back.

Flint turned away. *Served him right.*

'Get in the pickup.'

'Wait here.'

Flint wiped the condensation off the inside of the windscreen and watched Dad limp into the darkness. Wait here. Wait there. Do this. Do that. Gruff orders. Day in and day out. It was like living in his own private prison camp. Hard, back-breaking work, interspersed with long

8

spells of boredom and *this*, the nerve-racking stuff.

No time of his own. No freedom. Lousy food. A house with no furniture: nothing but rooms full of junk, empty clutter and things in boxes. And, of course, no clothes – perhaps the worst aspect of living with Dad, because the most embarrassing. God knows what people thought. T-shirts, jeans, *underwear*, whatever – as far as Dad was concerned, you wore them till they *wore out*. And then second-hand stuff would do.

The Foreign Legion might be friendlier. Certainly, it would be cosier and more comfortable. Being ruled by a permanently bad-tempered, tight-fisted tyrant and stranger, who *hated* football to boot – could anything be worse?

Running away to live on the streets, then dying of frostbite. That would be worse. Pictures he'd once seen in a magazine even now remained vivid in his memory: two boys, just a few years older than him, frozen to death in a shop doorway.

It needed warmer, drier weather, and money. So he was saving. Penny by penny. Stealing from Dad wasn't easy. It was *painfully* slow. But summer was still a *long* way off . . .

There was a tap on the window. Flint opened the door.

'Right.' Dad nodded towards the ugly, squat building. 'Ready to go.'

Pulling on his gloves, Flint followed his dad into the cold, drizzly night. A potholed street, ancient-looking street lamps, two of which weren't even working – the area was practically derelict. At a glance, you wouldn't think there could be anything here worth having.

At the side of the building, where the warehouse pressed close to its taller neighbour, there was a narrow seam, a slim alley running between the two.

'Down there.' Dad pointed the torch.

Flint peered. From both buildings, pipes of various sizes protruded into the alley. The torchlight bobbed between obstructions, before settling on a crate, propped against the wall.

'See?'

Flint nodded.

The light hit the wall and spread. It climbed. At a small dark cavity it stopped.

'That's it,' growled Dad. He handed Flint the torch.

Droplets flashed through the beam. Flint pulled his collar tighter. 'Here goes, then.'

'Wait.' The big hand gripped his shoulder. 'Run through, again.'

'Climb in. Locate bolt-cutters. Out the office, turn left into corridor. Double doors, first right into main warehouse. Straight through warehouse to main loading doors round the back. Bolts both sides at the bottom. You'll be waiting.'

Dad pressed a button on his watch. 'Fifteen minutes.'

'*What!* To load the pickup and *everything*?'

Dad nodded. 'I'll be round the back in five. *Move it!*'

Knocking into pipes as he hurried, Flint felt the ankle-deep water soaking through his trainers. Water dripping from the pipes seeped inside his collar. A mobile security patrol could be arriving in fifteen *seconds* for all he cared. This job couldn't be over fast enough.

The crate on the ground turned out to be an air-conditioning unit. Dad had ripped it from its sturdy steel housing on the warehouse wall. Clambering up, Flint reached for the hole in the brickwork. Stretched on his toes, his fingers barely touched.

He was on his own. Shoving the torch down the back of his trousers, he tucked the legs into his socks, stepped back to the edge of the air-conditioning unit, and *leapt*.

A heave, a kick and a frantic scramble – he was up, poking his head through the narrow hole.

Not a speck of light.

The shoulders took patience. Then you had to wriggle and push. *It was too tight*. The more he thrashed, the further the torch got pressed down his trousers. Finally, arms outstretched, he dropped into blackness, hit something hard and rolled.

No time to nurse injuries. Flint recovered the torch from his trouser leg and located the massive bolt-cutters. Any minute now Dad would be rattling the shutters.

Dragging the cutters, he hurried from the office, torch-beam sweeping. *Where were the swing doors?* His heart was racing. *Something was wrong*. He'd sensed it the moment they parked. Even in the dark, the building didn't feel right. It looked too run-down. Too messy. And the *smell* – it was musty, *damp*. The kind of gear they were after – *it wouldn't get stored in a place like this*.

Through the swing doors and out into the warehouse, the torch flickered across aisles of shelves, each stacked with boxes from floor to ceiling. Halfway down the first, Flint stopped and stared. Televisions. On the side of a box, next to the manufacturer's name and logo, a single scrawled word was caught in the beam: FAULTY.

Faulty! Flint jumped the beam to another box. FAULTY. The next: DEFECTIVE. Box after box, all the way to the end of the aisle. FAULTY. RETURNED. DEFECTIVE GOODS.

The warehouse was silent as a morgue. But, in his head, alarms were clanging, ringing, bleeping . . . He hurried to the next aisle – computers, according to the labels. But the same damning words were scrawled on the boxes: FAULTY, DEFECTIVE, RETURNED.

The shutter doors rattled. Flint could hear Dad growling his name. He hurried with the heavy-duty cutters. They bit through the bolts like scissors snipping curls.

He rapped on the shutters.

On the other side Dad grunted. The rollers creaked and the big metal shutters clattered up. Dim amber light flooded the warehouse.

'You're *late*.' Dad snatched the torch, and made straight for the boxes.

'I . . .' Flint scurried behind. 'I think someone's made a mistake.'

Dad scowled, box in hands. 'What?'

'Look.' Flint tapped cardboard. 'FAULTY – all the boxes are the same.'

'*What!*'

'The warehouse is full of the stuff,' said Flint. 'I checked other aisles.'

The box dropped from Dad's hands, hitting the floor with a *crash*. 'Which aisles?' He dragged Flint by the sleeve. 'Show me!'

Flint pointed.

Dad cursed. 'Check the others!' He handed back the torch. 'We're not leaving empty-handed.'

Flint hurried along the aisles. Every box bore the tell-tale words. He knew he was wasting his time. He knew what he'd find. *How could Dad have made such a blunder?*

Halfway down the third aisle Flint stopped dead in his tracks. *What was that?*

14

A car door, slamming. He clicked off the torch. A few aisles away Dad cursed in the gloom.

Someone, whistling a tune, rattled the doors at the front of the building.

Flint padded softly back along the aisle.

'We're leaving,' hissed Dad, looming out of the dark. 'In the pickup – *now!*'

CHAPTER 2
RIVER VIEW

A warehouse full of returned and faulty goods. A security patrol that turned up early. A getaway vehicle that failed to start. The warehouse job had been a series of disasters. No — a series of *first-class* disasters.

The security guards had actually been tapping on the pickup window by the time the engine finally spluttered into life. Then the mad movie car-chase. Dad swearing, swerving and running red lights. Credit where credit's due, he *had* eventually managed to shake the security guards and the police . . . in the early hours of the morning. And finally, having disposed of the false plates, they'd driven home and crawled to bed.

The catalogue of disasters might have ended there. But the following morning when Dad peeped through the blind, two men in a nondescript blue car were sitting outside the squat. He'd needed no further proof. The cops had finally tracked him down.

Not for the first time in recent history, home and everything in it had been abandoned.

And here they were. Not a squat this time. A caravan. One of those big, boxy ones, permanently berthed. A caravan park by a marina. The river just a stone's throw away. And trees.

River View.

'Hello.'

Flint stared. Beautiful flowers, all golds and yellows. A warm smile. Straight, fair hair, framing a pale, pretty face. She was tallish and slim. No makeup that he could see. Woman, or girl?

He nodded in greeting. There were small lines around her eyes, nothing deep like those etched beneath Dad's. Her irises were Man City blue.

'You must be Flint.'

17

'Must I?'

The smile broadened, the lines deepened. *'Definitely.'*

She squinted. 'Same features as him. Lighter colouring.'

Flint felt the eyes running over him from head to foot, and back again.

'Of course, you've still got some growing to do.' Her laugh was light and musical. 'But the suspicious manner's a *dead* giveaway! Your father's son, without a doubt.'

'Thanks!' Flint scowled. 'You've made my day.'

'Oops!' The woman bit her lip. 'Did I say the wrong thing?'

Flint shrugged.

'Is he in?'

Flint shook his head. 'Should be back soon.'

Putting one foot up on the step, the woman offered him the bouquet. 'These are for the caravan.'

'Oh . . . er . . . thanks.' Flint took the flowers awkwardly.

'I'm Saff.'

Flint nodded.

Her eyes studied his. 'He hasn't told you about me, has he?'

'Told what?'

She shook her head. 'Typical.'

'He tends to keep thoughts to himself.'

Saff gestured towards the step. 'D'you mind if I wait?'

Flint shrugged. 'I'd invite you in, only . . .'

'Don't worry.' The eyes twinkled. 'It's a nice enough day. I'm happy waiting here. You could keep me company.' She patted the step.

Laying the flowers on the ground, Flint sat down beside her.

'I'm living at the marina,' said Saff.

'On a boat?'

Saff nodded.

'Cool.'

'You'll have to come and visit.' Saff fiddled with the zip on her jacket. 'I thought your dad might have mentioned it.'

Flint shook his head.

'We were at school together,' said Saff. 'But he was a few years above me. We became friends after.'

'Were you boyfriend and girlfriend?'

Saff nodded. 'For a short time. Before . . .' She hesitated. '. . . he met your mother.'

Flint looked away.

'I'm sorry . . . You must still be . . .'

He took a deep, shuddering breath. His eyes pricked.

19

'That wasn't very sensitive of me.' Saff touched his shoulder.

He sniffed. 'I feel stupid.'

'Don't.' The hand squeezed. 'Here.'

A tissue. He took it and blew his nose.

'It must have been awful for you . . . your dad told me how she died.'

Flint tried to shrug. His breath shuddered again.

'Then having to move in with *him* – that *can't* have been easy.'

Flint sucked his lip between his teeth; wiped his eyes.

'He's very changed, from the man I first knew.'

'We only met twice.' Flint turned. 'Before Mum died.'

Saff's mouth dropped.

Flint nodded. 'Once when I was four. And again when I was seven. Perhaps there were a few other times, when I was a baby.' He shrugged. 'But they don't really count. Dad abandoned us because we didn't fit in with his plans. That's what Mum told me.'

'Have you talked to him about it?'

'You're kidding! Dad doesn't talk about that stuff.'

Saff shook her head. 'He's so different . . .

so different to the man I used to know.'

'Talk of the devil.'

Bouncing the dirty white pickup over the hump in the drive, Dad parked and climbed out. He nodded stiffly to Saff. 'Wasn't expecting you.'

'She brought us flowers,' said Flint. He scooped up the bouquet.

Dad frowned.

'Don't worry.' Saff smiled. 'I won't disrupt things.' She rose to her feet. 'I just thought I'd pop by, to see how you're settling.'

Flint handed the flowers to his father.

'Thanks.' Dad looked embarrassed and shuffled from foot to foot. 'They're . . . nice.' He opened the caravan door. 'Things are a bit disorganized . . . we could probably manage coffee . . .'

'They need putting in water,' said Saff, mounting the steps. 'I don't suppose you've got a vase . . . ?' She stepped inside.

Dad turned to Flint. 'Take a walk.' He tossed a coin out towards the drive. 'Do some exploring.'

The caravan door slammed shut.

CHAPTER 3
RUBBISH FOOTBALLER

It was the first time Dad had given him money. His mouth watered. Sweets, chocolates – *think what he could buy*. It had to go to the escape fund, of course. But that wasn't going to stop him fantasizing about the *luxuries* of his previous life. Before things had turned so grey. So hard.

The riverbank was dotted with anglers, the path was busy with families, couples and people walking dogs. Beyond the marina the river meandered past an industrial estate, then streets of derelict houses and big warehouse buildings. A big, battered sign advertised to passing river traffic: DODGE THE SCRAP – KEN DODGE: BREAKERS & SCRAP MERCHANTS.

After the scrapyard there were more houses and warehouses. Then the river turned sharply, almost doubling back on itself. The type of houses changed. Streets of terraces running end-on to the river gave way to bigger, older houses, which looked out across it, singly and in pairs. As the houses got larger, so did the gardens.

He had lost track of how long he'd been walking, or how far he'd walked. He had come to a gate. Beyond, a huge grassy space opened out, stretching back from the river and its footpath, like a village green. Houses with high walls, hedges and trees edged the space, grander by far than any he had passed. A church clock and spire stood proud above them.

His mood had been rising. Distance from Dad always felt good. And now – he shivered, a sudden spasm of excitement – in the middle of the common: a group of boys were playing *football*.

Blood pumped.

The players' voices rang out. The game was fast. A mixture of talents. Some individual flair, but little sign of teamwork. They communicated well. But there was tension.

'Come on!' Arrogant vowels. 'Push it

through!' Rich, a strong-looking boy with dark hair, was doing most of the shouting. He was captaining the side that was behind. He liked to wait up front for scoring opportunities. He rebuked far more than he encouraged. He had six other players. The other side had one less.

Slighter, freckled and fairer, a boy called Josh led the opposition. Constantly switching between attack and defence, he made it his personal responsibility to mark Rich. He *worked* at his team's motivation.

A wild pass got through to Rich. Two metres from the keeper, he spectacularly miskicked. The goalie went the wrong way and the ball trickled between the two cones that were posts. Players turned to the church clock, examined their watches.

The game became frantic.

Flint chewed a fingernail. A real football. In good condition too. He hadn't kicked a football since . . . Mum. An old tennis ball, the odd tin can or piece of rubbish, tapped back and forth on the sly. And, of course, the fantasy games in his head. But as far as footballs went, he was totally *starved*!

'*Yes!*' bellowed Rich. 'With only seconds to spare, he does it again! *Goal!*' He leapt, punching the air over and over. His team, goalie included, gave chase. As they cavorted and celebrated, the church clock began to chime. 'Full time!' yelled Rich. 'Four-all!'

Josh's face looked drawn. His team downcast.

'Five minutes' rest,' panted Rich. 'Then it's golden goals.'

'The first team to score, wins.'

Suddenly, all the boys were shouting at once. Flint moved closer to catch what was said.

'That's not fair! The sides aren't equal.'

'You weren't complaining before.'

'It's different now!'

'Now you're not winning.'

'Yeah.'

'Tough! One of your team had to go off. There's no way we're giving up a player to even things out. Too bad there's no-one left for you to pick.'

Josh nudged a mate and motioned towards Flint. Slipping away from the argument, the two boys headed over.

Flint tensed. *Where would be the harm, if they asked him to join?* Dad wasn't going to know. He was miles away. Preoccupied.

Josh nodded a greeting. 'We're stuck for a player.'

'Marcus,' said the chubby-faced boy, introducing himself. 'Any good at football?'

'Flint.' Flint shrugged. 'Bit rusty.'

The two teammates glanced at one another.

'Could be rubbish,' muttered Marcus. 'We might be better off without. He's not much to look at.'

Flint chewed his lip. It'd been a long time since he'd met boys his own age. Dad had seen to that. He felt edgy.

'Beggars can't be choosers.' Josh squinted at Flint, as though trying to spot tell-tale signs of a rubbish footballer. 'You *have* played before?'

Flint nodded. 'Just not recently.'

The two teammates exchanged glances.

'Beggars can't be choosers.' Marcus sighed. 'You said it.'

Flint glanced towards the other boys.

'Everyone's knackered,' said Josh. 'Apart from André, all of us have played the full ninety. But Rich and his boys hit a winning streak after Nicholas had to go off. *Their* spirits are soaring. We're desperate. We need a lift.'

'It's sudden death next,' said Marcus.

26

'One goal and it's over.'

'What do you think?' Josh gestured towards the arguing players. 'You've watched us – reckon you can make a difference?'

Flint shrugged. 'I'll have a go.'

'OK.'

Voices fell as the three of them returned to the group. All eyes turned on Flint. Weighing him up. All the boys were wearing quality clothes, quality trainers – he had noticed that straightaway. The kind of gear he used to wear when Mum had bought his clothes; Dad only allowed him cheap stuff. *How would they see him, in his old jeans and clapped out trainers?*

Rich's gaze was steely. 'Who's this?' he sneered.

'Yeah – who is he?' echoed someone.

'Flint.' Josh put a hand on Flint's shoulder. There were mutters and glances. 'Flint,' said Josh, 'is replacing Nicholas. He's our seventh man.'

'You can't bring on a player after full time,' said Rich.

'Why not?' said Marcus. 'You brought on André to even up the numbers.'

'That's different,' said Rich. 'The game had only just started. Anyway, André

27

plays for the club.' He pointed at Flint.
'Who's *this*? No-one knows him.'

Marcus folded his arms. 'So?'

'He could be anybody.'

'What – like a ringer?' Marcus chuckled.
'Worried we might still beat you?'

Flint's skin prickled under the scrutiny.
Rich pointed. 'Worried by *that*?' He
threw back his head and laughed. His
teammates joined him. 'You've got to be
joking!'

'Good.' Josh nodded. 'You've got seven.
Now, so have we. That's fair.'

'No more whingeing.' Rich cracked his
knuckles. 'Let battle commence!'

Flint was too tense. The first couple of
times the ball came near him, he totally
fluffed it. A bald tennis ball had been the
last thing he'd kicked; a full-size football
felt enormous. Too big to miss – but he'd
still managed to, both times. It was nerves
and excitement.

There was little strategy on either side.
Both teams were tired and, after a few
early runs to snatch a quick victory, they
settled back to defensive play. Any attempt
by one side to push forward, opposition
players fell back to block their efforts.

Marcus sliced the ball, straight to the opposition.

'Keep your concentration!' yelled Josh.

Play switched direction. Rich embarked on his third solo onslaught. On the wing, Flint hurried to catch the rest of his side, now all in retreat.

Rich was taller than everyone on the pitch and used his size to intimidate. He was fast too, even after ninety minutes' slog. 'Here I come,' he yelled, barging past Marcus. 'Ready or not.'

But Flint was fresher and faster. At full tilt, he raced up the wing, cutting in towards the goal. He slowed to a jog.

One against six, Rich bore down on the goal, overtaking players. Josh and a red-head called Chris positioned themselves to intercept. But Rich had built up a ton of speed. He leapt Josh's tackle, knocking him to the ground, then niftily dodged round Chris.

A wide gap opened between Rich and the goal. Only the keeper stood in his way.

'Flint!' yelled Josh. 'Block him.'

Flint charged.

The keeper was staying back on his line. Rich manoeuvred to shoot.

Hurling himself, Flint slid along the

ground. The ball flew clear. He bounced to his feet. Behind him, Rich cursed and thudded to the ground. The ball was rolling to Marcus.

'Go on!' yelled Josh.

Marcus punted back to Flint.

'Man on!' yelled his captain.

Rich was on his feet and charging like a bull. Flint twisted and ducked a reckless arm. Rich lunged and lost his balance. Tapping the ball to Josh, Flint skipped over Rich and pushed forwards.

Josh kicked it back. 'Go, Flint, go!' he yelled.

Flint tore up the middle of the pitch, arms pumping, legs churning. *Effortless.* He was in the game, he had contributed at last. The old skills – the judgement, the timing, the *nerve* – they had all come together. It was still there. He lofted the ball to the wing. 'Marcus!'

Marcus chased it.

Flint felt giddy with excitement. A blazing fireball, carried forward by his own momentum, he streaked into enemy territory.

The opposition were clustered in front of the goal.

'Flint!' Marcus passed low, a touch of curve.

Flint had outrun his weary teammates. No time to wait for backup. Praying that luck and the skills would stay with him, he cut right with the ball, drawing opposition players away from the goal.

They came for him.

He slowed, feigning indecision. 'Come on!' he taunted, tempting them out further. 'Come and get it!'

Two players took the bait.

He surged again, chipping over their heads, blazing between them and chasing it. He controlled the ball, twisted to give a third man the slip, then, arriving in front of goal . . . *blasted* it.

With the game over, arguments began. Voices rose. Flint nodded his goodbye, and slipped away to the river.

'Hey!'

Flint kept walking.

Feet pounded the ground behind him. 'That was quite a goal.'

'Thanks.' He kept walking.

'I don't think Rich was too pleased.' Josh panted and chuckled. 'He doesn't like to be beaten.'

'No?'

'He's the club's top goal-scorer. He's

used to having things his own way.'

Flint kept his eyes on the footpath. 'I can imagine.'

'You don't say much, do you?'

Flint shrugged. 'Sorry.' He'd reached the gate.

Josh got his hand to the latch. 'It was cool playing with you,' he said. He made a fist.

Flint made his own and touched it to Josh's. He smiled.

Josh smiled back. 'Perhaps you'll come down again?'

'Maybe.'

The gate swung open.

CHAPTER 4
SAME OLD

Flint stared glumly at passing streets. Same old same old. A city full of houses, full of boys and girls his own age he was never going to meet. They all went to school. They had lots of friends their own age. They played games of football he would never get to join.

Little had changed since the move. Same life, different city. Hard up again. Collecting scrap again. The only thing missing was the break-ins. But they would come; it was just a matter of time. Just a matter of Dad setting up contacts and sussing the lie of the land. It'd happened last time they moved. And the time before that.

He glanced across at Dad, rolling a cigarette as he steered.

Same Dad – the Dad who hated football with a black bitterness. Nothing was guaranteed to get his blood boiling quicker. Sneaking a kick was practically impossible. Grass-stained jeans from the village green game had aroused his deepest suspicions. He'd been on the alert ever since.

Dad's fingers drummed on the wheel. The pickup slowed. A betting shop in sight. He lit his cigarette, dragged deeply and coughed. The low rumble in his chest was as much a part of him as the limp, and the five-o'clock shadow.

He changed gear. The betting shop drifted past. He coughed again, hawked and spat into the street.

Taking a left, they picked up speed on a clear stretch of road and filtered onto a dual-carriageway. Flint wound down the window to enjoy the breeze. It was the end of a day, the tail-end of a wearying week.

A flyover took them up above trees and houses, revealing a brief glimpse of the river before dropping them back to the ground. The pickup stopped at lights.

Flint dangled his arm from the window. Wasn't there *anything* good to be said for a life with Dad? Changes of address and riding every day in the pickup meant he'd seen a lot of places. He knew his way round several towns and cities. *That* might be useful.

'Marcus!'

Flint froze. Laughing and joking, a group of boys in school uniform crossed the road. A football was being passed back and forth. There was no mistaking the faces and voices.

'Marcus, you gonk.' Rich beckoned. '*Pass* it.'

'Get lost.' Marcus tapped the ball to Josh.

Rich swivelled towards Josh. '*Pass!*'

Josh scowled.

'Come on! *Pass* it.'

Josh back-heeled to the boy behind.

Flint lowered his head.

'*Wuss!*' snorted Rich. 'Wuss-in-boots!'

'Can't you give it a rest?'

Rich laughed. '*Ahhh* . . . you can't take it, can you, Josh-u-ah?' His tone sharpened. 'That's why I'm captain. And you're not.'

The pickup pulled away.

*   *   *

DODGE THE CRAP. Flint chuckled. The sign overlooking the entrance was well-weathered. It had faded. The s had clearly been missing for some time.

Dad glowered. 'What's so funny?'

Flint shrugged. *Dad never joked.*

The pickup bowled through the gates and shuddered to a stop beside a small, battered caravan. The word OFFICE was scrawled on a piece of cardboard over the front window.

In a flash, a pack of fierce, scrappy-looking dogs were tearing round the pickup. They yapped and barked, jumping and snapping at the windows in a wolfish frenzy.

'All right, girls!' A huge voice boomed across the yard, followed by a shrill whistle.

Instantly, the dogs were transformed into tail-wagging friends.

'They're customers, you silly beggars. They're *mates*.' Ken Dodge beamed and waved. Filthy stained T-shirt, stretched tight by enormous belly; walrus moustache, topped by sun-polished dome. He was massive. 'Welcome, gents!'

Flint opened the door. Two sets of paws landed on his lap, two shaggy mongrel faces sniffed and licked his own. He patted the snouts.

'*Sporty . . . Ginger . . .*' Ken's tone bristled with threat. '*Down!*'

Sad-eyed, the dogs whined and backed away. Flint clambered out, pleased for an opportunity to stretch at last.

Shaking hands like the old friends they were, Dad and Ken leaned against the pick-up. Dad took out his tobacco. Ken looked in the back. 'What you brought for me, then?'

Dad spat in the dirt and shook his head. 'A week's worth of hard graft, that is.'

'Perhaps you've been trying the wrong places.'

'Pah!' Dad banged the side. 'It's this lousy town, this lousy country, this—'

'Whoa!' Ken put a hand loosely on Dad's shoulders. 'It can't be *that* bad . . .' He chuckled. 'Let's have a look.'

Flint looked around at the yard. Old cars piled in blocks . . . six, seven, *eight* cars high, many still recognizable, in spite of severe distortions. No apparent order to the stacking. Some so precariously balanced, the slightest touch might bring them crashing.

A scruffy terrier yapped, turned tail and raced off between walls of cars. An

Alsatian and a Dobermann trotted lazily behind, sniffing and ferreting. Flint followed. The collie and the Labrador, who had already befriended him, hung back in his company.

Underfoot, the soil was tacky with oil. Peppered with nuts, bolts and other small parts, it sparkled with broken glass. Flint kicked at a chunk of orange plastic, the shattered remains of an indicator. He whacked it. It soared, ricocheted and disappeared.

Suddenly, there was a commotion ahead. The Alsatian and the Dobermann stopped in their tracks and barked. Dashing between them, the terrier galloped wild-eyed, a blue ball clenched between her small jaws. The two larger dogs gave chase, the others yapped excitedly. The ball wasn't much smaller than the terrier's head. Flint couldn't help laughing.

Slamming on the brakes, she dropped it in front of Flint. The other dogs collided.

Flint bent. 'Want me to chuck it for you?' He reached towards the ball.

The terrier growled and snapped.

'Uh-oh!' Flint froze. 'Maybe you don't . . .'

Dropping her head, the terrier butted the ball.

'Ah!' Flint caught it with his toe. *'That's* what you want to play!' He flicked.

Three dogs leapt into the air, clashed, barking and snapping. As the ball dropped, the terrier butted and ran.

'Slick!' Flint stuck out a foot to obstruct her.

But with a series of short, sharp turns, the terrier squeezed past and took off.

'Oi!' Flint swivelled. 'Cheeky!'

The other dogs had scrambled in pursuit. Flint gave chase. The terrier was fast, but no match for the others. Size and agility were her advantage. Every time one of her pursuers overtook, she slammed on the brakes and doubled back through their legs. She could accelerate, and she could turn on a coin. Again and again she got away.

Panting for breath, Flint clutched himself. He laughed, helpless, as the terrier shot through his legs, still butting the ball.

'Aaaaagh!'

Flint span round. That was *Dad*. It sounded like pain. *Serious* pain.

He ran. The dogs stared as he tore past into the clearing. Dad was sprawled. Upended on the ground between him and the pickup lay a heavy old cooker. Four of them had struggled to load it the previous day.

Ken offered an arm.

'I'm all right!' Dad waved him away.

'You wanna watch that leg of yours.'

Using the cooker for support, Dad heaved himself jerkily to his feet. He gasped as he straightened up. 'It's not my leg.'

'Well – whatever.' Ken shrugged. 'You wanna take care.'

'Easier said than done.'

'Have a little think . . .' Ken paused, noticing Flint. He tapped the side of his nose. '. . . think about *what we said.*'

'You all right, Dad?'

Dad turned, wincing. He scowled. 'Where were *you*?'

Saff's hand hovered by his plate. 'You're quite sure you've had enough?'

Flint nodded.

'There's still more if you want it. I made plenty.'

'I'm really stuffed. Thanks. Fantastic spag.'

'Bolognese is one of my specialities.' Saff added Flint's plate to the two she was

40

clutching. 'Want to give me a hand? You could clear the other things whilst I make the coffee.'

From the outside, the boat had looked narrow and cramped. But inside, it was tidy, brightly decorated, and surprisingly spacious. Flint collected up the glasses and carried them through. A partition and bead curtains separated the kitchen from the dining area. The pattern on the partition matched the curtains.

'Like it?' said Saff. 'I'm making you hot chocolate.'

'Thanks.' Flint nodded. 'Did you paint it?'

'Yep.' Saff grinned. 'Everything you can see.' She waved a hand. 'After I'd refitted the whole boat, from top to bottom.'

'Wow! That must have taken ages.'

Saff nodded. 'About a year. A bit here, a bit there, in between painting jobs. My carpentry skills are self-taught and I'm still a little slow.' She tapped one of the intricately painted doors that led to the rear of the boat. *Dawn Treader* taught me a lot. But I'm still not confident enough carpentry-wise to do other people's boats.'

'The painting looks brilliant.'

'Thank you. You help your dad with

his business . . . ? Is that good?'

'I suppose.' Flint felt awkward suddenly. Saff was warm, her eyes promised trust, but she was Dad's friend, not his. 'Dad needs me,' he said, looking away.

'But you're too young, surely?' Saff poured the pan of steaming milk into three cups. 'You should still be at school.'

'You don't have to,' said Flint. 'It's not illegal if your parents don't send you.'

'Maybe.' Carrying the cups on a tray, Saff backed through the bead curtain. Flint followed. 'Parents can be prosecuted,' said Saff, 'if they fail to educate their children.'

Dad humphed dismissively. 'The boy's getting an education.'

Saff scowled as she handed Dad his coffee. 'What have you taught him, then? Apart from where to look for scrap.' Her face tightened. 'How to break into people's homes? How to recognize what's worth stealing?' She turned to Flint. 'He's taken you with him on his burglaries, hasn't he?'

Flint stared. She knew. What was he supposed to say? He glanced at Dad.

'Don't worry,' said Saff. 'You can tell me the truth, he doesn't mind.' She glared at Dad. 'Do you?'

Dad shook his head. 'Go ahead,' he said.

His lip curled. 'Tell Saff what you like.'

Flint gripped his mug. The crazy urge to just blurt out everything was very strong. Tell it *all* to Saff. Then she could help him, *rescue* him. But that wasn't going to happen – if he tried to say the wrong things, Dad would silence him. He sipped his hot chocolate. 'I've been on a few of those jobs.'

Saff sat down next to Dad. 'Well, not any more.' She draped a skinny arm across his shoulders. 'Your father's made a promise.' She touched his chest. 'No more nicking tellies and stuff . . .'

Dad stared at the coffee. His face twitched.

'Isn't that right?' said Saff. Dad forced a nod.

'No more warehouse jobs . . .'

He nodded again and leant forward to sip his drink. Suddenly, his whole body jerked. Coffee spilled. He *yelled*, as hot liquid hit his lap. The cup clattered under the table.

'God!' Grabbing a crumpled serviette, Saff dabbed at his trousers. 'Are you *all right*?'

Dad tried to stand; he gasped and sat back. 'The coffee was too hot!'

'The coffee?' Saff frowned. 'Don't be silly! It's the same as mine.'

'Yours must have more milk.'

Saff halted mid-action. 'It hadn't touched your lips.'

Dad winced.

'Something happened this afternoon,' said Flint. He'd seen Dad swallow extra painkillers before they left the caravan.

Dad scowled.

'I think . . .' Flint hesitated. 'Dad hurt himself . . . shifting a cooker.'

'The back again?' said Saff.

Dad shook his head. 'It was just a muscle.' He rubbed his thigh. 'Nothing a couple of aspirin won't sort.'

Saff touched his hand. 'I'll get you your aspirin,' she said. 'But tomorrow – no argument – you and I are visiting the doctor.'

CHAPTER 5
FOOTBALL

Flint made his way towards the players.

'Nicholas!' Rich bellowed from the front. 'To your left. *To your left!*'

The slight midfielder glanced up too late.

Marcus skinned him and took off, laughing. 'Cheers!'

'You big lettuce!' snapped Rich. 'D'you plan on being pathetic *all* your life?'

There was more laughter as Marcus charged unhindered towards the other end. The game proper hadn't started yet. The boys were still warming up, playing around.

Rich was first to spot Flint. 'Well – *look*

who it is.' His tone was sneering. *'Mystery boy.'*

Flint nodded greeting.

'Excellent!' Josh grinned. 'Just in time. That gives us equal numbers.'

Rich grunted. 'He turns up, scores the flukiest goal ever, then sneaks off. Back to *wherever*. No *thanks, guys,* no *goodbye.'*

Boys stared. Flint felt himself shrinking.

'That's rubbish!' said Josh. 'We were all busy bickering, no-one would have noticed. Frankly, I'm amazed he bothered to come back. Come on. Who are you going to pick: André or Flint?'

Flint smiled at the situation: Rich looking from him to André and back again, pretending to be making up his mind.

'I'll stick with what I can rely on,' said Rich. 'Over here, André. With the winners.'

Josh beckoned to Flint.

André strode over to his captain with smug poise. Flint mocked with a swagger. Behind their own captain, Marcus and Justin, the goalie, laughed. Flint recognized other players. The sides had divided up pretty much as before.

The two teams huddled around their captains.

'We have to be flexible,' said Josh.

'Constantly on the alert. Looking to cover for each other, as well as doing our own job.' He turned to Flint. 'You and I are going to chop a hole through their defence.'

They moved to their places, ready for kick-off.

Josh touched Flint's elbow. 'When you didn't show up, I thought we'd seen the last of you.'

Flint shrugged. 'It was tricky . . . getting away.'

By the end of the first half Josh's side were 3–1 down. Their only goal had been Flint's.

The game had been far more one-sided than the scoreline revealed. Rich's team had applied constant pressure. Flint and Josh had rarely received passes up front. Over and again, they'd been forced to come right back, to dig out the ball for themselves.

Flint was itching for a good break.

Josh addressed his gathered team. 'The defence is just not gelling.'

'We need another man,' said Justin. 'By the time they reach our back line, they've got too much momentum. We can't afford both of you up front.'

'Yeah.' Josh nodded. 'You're right. I'm

going to hang back this half. Flint, you'll
have to take care of the attack. We'll try to
rig a tighter defence.' He patted him on the
back. 'Nice goal. Can you manage a few
more this half?'

'Feed me.' Flint grinned. 'And see.'

The church bell chimed.

'OK!' bellowed Rich. 'Time's up, losers.
Coming, ready or not!'

'Let's do it!' yelled Josh.

Flint sprinted. Nicholas kicked off,
tapping it back to his captain. Rich punted
wide to André on the wing. André waited
for Flint to come close, before chipping
back to his captain.

Flint chased and leapt as Rich
attempted the volley. 'Mine!' He blocked
... staggered.

Rich's face darkened with rage.

Flint took off, weaving his way round
challengers, Rich on his tail.

'*Go*, Flint!' yelled Josh. 'Turbo-drive! All
the way!'

Defenders fell aside. The goal opened up
in front of him, the keeper yelling and
waving from his line. Flint accelerated.

'Yaaaaaaaaaaaah!' The keeper tore out
to meet him.

'Yaaaaaaaaaaaaah!' Lowering his head,

Flint charged like a bull. Straight for goal. He lurched.

The keeper sprang, stretching through the air in a great shot-blocking dive. But it was the wrong way: the toe-poked ball had already passed him. It rolled gently between the posts.

'*Yeeeeees!*' shrieked Josh.

'The jammy basket.' Rich booted a piece of turf. 'Scoring from a miskick – he does it again!'

'An opinion from our expert!' Josh chuckled.

'Get stuffed!' Rich glared. 'Beginner's luck runs out.'

Flint smiled.

Rich turned to the keeper. 'What are you waiting for, peabrain? *Fetch the ball.* You're wasting valuable time.'

Flint ran back into his half.

Rich took the kick this time, tapping the ball back to his midfield. The second his foot touched the ball, Flint was running, *searing* past. He'd sussed Rich's plan – to push forward with his midfield following close behind. He knew Rich's defenders would be able to see him coming; they'd have time to pick their player and loft the ball. Almost too much time.

He had the X factor – fresh goal-scorer's nerve and momentum. It unsettled defenders. Turned them dithery. It made all the difference . . .

'Man on!' Rich's voice bellowed from the other end of the pitch. 'Gavin! Get rid of it!'

The short defender stared at Flint, open-mouthed.

In one swift movement, Flint hooked the ball away and swerved towards goal. The keeper stiffened. Shouted at his defenders. But already it was too late. Flint was travelling with such speed, they weren't going to catch him. It was one on one. He kept running, running.

Close enough to see the keeper's sweat, he dummied another toe-poker. The keeper dropped and . . .

Flint cruelly chipped.

'*Beautiful!*' Josh ran towards him, arms outstretched like a glider.

'Excellent shot!' Marcus kicked the air, laughing.

Behind them, Rich scowled. He muttered and spat at the ground.

'Sorry, didn't quite catch that, Mister Expert.' Josh chuckled, turning. 'What's your opinion – *more* beginner's luck?'

Flint patted the keeper on the back. 'Nice try.'

'Yeah, thanks!' said the goalie. 'Not so bad yourself.'

Flint froze.

Other boys had already turned to look. 'Mad woman on a bicycle!' said Rich.

Riding along the towpath, hair billowing in the breeze, Saff smiled, waved and whistled.

'Who's she?' said Josh.

'Never seen her before,' said Marcus.

'Me neither,' said the keeper.

Flint screwed his eyes shut. *Please let her vanish*. He opened them.

Saff waved. *She had recognized him*. She would tell Dad.

'Escaped from somewhere,' said Rich.

'She was whistling at you,' chuckled Marcus.

Rich scowled. 'This is time-wasting. Get back in your own half. We're taking the kick.' Snatching the ball from the keeper, he set off, running towards the centre.

'Come on!' yelled Josh.

Shaking himself, Flint hurried.

He was fast. He was there in front of Rich, when he put the ball down on the centre spot. But . . . *what was going to happen when he got home?* Dad would go absolutely *ballistic*, that's what! If Saff told Dad she'd seen him playing, he'd totally *flip*. There was no crime more serious in his book.

He was in *big* trouble.

'Oi, *Flint!*' Josh, alarmed. 'Wakey-wakey!'

Flint span round. Rich must have dribbled right past him, and he was already scything his way through the midfield.

Two players tried to block, but Rich switched direction.

Marcus chased and harried, driving Rich further and further towards the wing. Several of Rich's team had moved up, and were finding good, deep positions, ready to receive.

Angry with himself, Flint fell back. Maybe he could still help.

Pursued by Marcus, Rich had been drawn out to the wing. As Josh moved to close him down, he searched for a chance to slip the ball away.

Flint slowed in the crowded goal area. *What if he shot off home?* He'd never catch Saff on her bicycle, obviously. But if he got a move on, he might see her before she

52

spoke to Dad. She might be going back to the boat. Somewhere else, even.

Players jostled for position. Suddenly, everyone in front of the goal was jumping. The ball was in the air and dropping.

Flint saw it too late. Coming straight for him. No time to jump. No time . . .

He jerked.

The ball glanced past Justin's shocked face. Inside the post.

He had scored again. Own goal.

'*Seven–three seven–three seven–three, seven–three seven–three seven–threeee!*'

With the mocking chorus ringing in his ears, Flint pulled up his hood and hurried towards the path. Rich had scored a few. No-one had played brilliantly, but *he* had played like a prize idiot: missing the ball, falling over, scoring an own goal . . . it was too humiliating!

'*Flint!*'

He speeded up.

'Flint – it's a *game*! Don't take it so *personally*.' Josh overtook him, panting. 'Come on!' He grinned. 'You had a good *first* half. And you started off well in the second . . . it's not as if you're the only one who cocked up.' He put a hand on Flint's

53

shoulder. 'Today was a bad day. But you still scored a couple of beauties. The scoreline would have been even more tragic without them.' He blocked Flint's path. 'Come on.'

Flint scowled and cut wide.

'Don't do your disappearing act again.' Josh blocked his path again, grinning.

Flint moved the other way.

'Please?' Josh barred with his arms. 'I know it's harder for you. We all know each other and you're, well . . . the outsider. But everyone has a lot of respect . . .' His arms lowered. 'I'm *not* just saying that.'

'Rich especially, right?'

'OK.' Josh made a face. 'Maybe not Rich. Rich is just a prat. Law of averages: you always get one in a group this size. The only person Rich can ever appreciate is himself. He's so *supremely* talented . . . He doesn't like it when someone shows him up.'

Flint smiled.

'You're good with the ball – *really* good, when things are right. And our club needs new blood.'

Flint halted. 'Club?'

'Beckton Leigh.' Josh nodded. 'YFC. Marcus, Justin – everybody. We play for the same team. It's only a small club. But Cup and League.'

'Rich, too?'

Josh groaned. 'Yeah – 'fraid so.'

'And what – you fancy yourself as a talent scout?'

Josh shrugged and smiled.

'Sorry.' Flint pushed past. 'Keep searching.'

Josh overtook, scurrying backwards. 'Who do you play for?'

'I don't.'

'Then why not play for us?'

'I wouldn't be *allowed*.'

'How d'you mean?' Josh stumbled. 'Why not?'

'You wouldn't understand. Your parents have probably encouraged you.' Flint paused in front of the gate. He shrugged. 'Others don't.'

Josh halted beside him. 'People can be persuaded.'

Flint pushed the gate. 'Believe me – some *can't*.'

Dad's eyes appeared to bulge in their sockets, but the explosion didn't materialize. 'You disobeyed me.' The words precisely measured.

Flint ducked his chin. 'The thing is . . .'

'*Shut* it!' Dad twisted, glaring at Saff. 'And *no* discussion.'

Saff stared at her fingers.

Flint coughed to clear the dryness from his throat. He was getting off lightly because Saff was present. Things would be different later. 'Some of them live in big posh houses.' He spoke quickly. 'Could be great for business.'

This was a gamble. Dad glowered. Saff raised her head. She smiled encouragingly.

'Quality scrap,' said Flint. 'It's been pretty poor pickings in this area, so far – right?'

Dad's face was stony.

'But these people probably have heaps of unwanted stuff just waiting to be collected.'

'You could get some business cards printed,' said Saff.

Dad's eyes flickered.

'There's probably odd jobs too,' said Flint. 'Bits of gardening, window-cleaning, that sort of thing. Once you get in with these sort, there could be no end of money to be made.'

Dad grunted. 'What are their names?'

Not the response he'd expected. 'Sorry?'

'Your new friends,' said Dad. 'These . . . *posh* boys.'

'Josh, Justin, Marcus . . . Richard, André . . .'

Dad nodded; almost smiled. 'Upper Beckton, yeah?'

Flint nodded. Was he being *wrong-footed*?

'The idea's brilliant,' said Saff. 'It couldn't have come at a better time.' She turned to Flint. 'Your dad doesn't like me interfering, I know — but the doctor's sending him for tests at the hospital. There's to be strictly no lifting till we get the results.'

She shuffled closer to Dad, patting his leg. 'It *could* be just a matter of pulled muscles. But, if it's the back injury reactivated, the doctor said *serious bad news*.'

Dad snorted and shook his head.

'You'll be the fool.' Saff frowned. 'It's no joking matter.'

CHAPTER 6
THAW

Standing outside his office, Ken petted the dogs. 'If you're not happy with the prices, you're welcome to try somewhere else.'

Dad scowled. 'Like I'm really going to – with the whole lot unloaded.'

Ken grinned, showing teeth full of gaps. 'You won't hurt my feelings.'

'Feelings?' Dad spat the word, heaving himself behind the wheel. He swore as he slammed the door, cursed as he started the engine.

Flint slumped in the seat. The end of another hard week. And Dad narked again at the amount of money they'd earned. With him unable to lift much, what did he expect?

Dad gunned the engine and span the back wheels, churning up a spray of oily dirt.

Roaring with laughter, Ken waved at this final, petulant gesture. 'Think about what I said.'

The pickup lurched through the gate and away down the street towards the ring-road.

Dad drove in sullen, tight-lipped silence. Nosing up too close to whatever got in the way, he used the horn like a gun, blasting every obstacle. Motorists pulled over to let him pass, pedestrians crossing the road ran for their lives.

Clutching his seat belt, Flint closed his eyes and tried to pretend the swoops, the swerves and lurches were part of a fairground ride. There was no use saying anything, it would only make things worse. Dad was in one of his moods. At least, if they didn't hit anything, they were going to be home early.

Gradually the swearing, the horn-blaring and engine-revving diminished. The radio clicked on, and the smell of tobacco mingled with the cocktail of traffic fumes. As the ride grew more comfortable, Flint felt himself slipping towards sleep. His eyelids had become too heavy to lift.

'Flint!'

Something jabbed him in the ribs. The Country and Western and the cigarette smoke had gone . . . so had the traffic fumes! Flint shook himself, sat up and rubbed his eyes. 'This isn't River View.'

'Give the boy a medal.'

The pickup was parked on a grass verge. On the other side of a low hedge, a golf-course stretched towards distant trees, houses and a church spire. Cheerfully sweatered golfers laughed and chatted, trundling their caddie carts.

Flint glanced at his father. 'You're not planning to take up golf?'

'That's right,' Dad grunted. 'I'm *not*.' He jerked his thumb towards the other side of the road. A neat brick building, and a long wall topped by a high wire fence. '*That's* why we're here.'

From where he was sitting, Flint could just make out a few letters on the sign: E–I–G–H . . . Y–F–C. The last three made his heart gallop. 'YFC – Youth Football Club! Is it *Beckton Leigh*?'

Dad shrugged and frowned. 'You never told me the name. I found the area, then drove around till I came across this place.

There can't be that many clubs in a neighbourhood like this.'

Expensive-looking cars lined the road. Flint spotted two boys he recognized from the village green games. They had just clambered out of a 4×4 and were hurrying towards the gate in the wall. He felt himself tensing. *Why had Dad brought him here? Was it part of some warped scheme to punish him? Was he planning some kind of public humiliation?*

'Could you find your way home?' Dad's expression seldom gave anything away.

Flint nodded. The spire was the one with a clock, which overlooked the green.

'Good.' Reaching across in front of Flint, Dad opened the passenger side door. 'Let's see.' He motioned towards the club. 'Go on.'

'The football club? Are you serious?'

Dad glared. 'Do I joke?'

'Never.'

'Well then . . .'

Flint bit his lip. There had to be a catch. 'I've no kit.'

'Let's see if they'll have you, first,' said Dad. 'You might not be good enough.'

Flint nodded. Dad had no idea. He'd never seen him play.

'Looks as if boys are turning up for a

practice of some sort,' said Dad. 'If you go over now, you might be able to scrounge something to play in. They might even give you a trial.'

Flint scrambled out.

'I'll have a smoke,' said Dad. 'If you're not back then, I'll assume you're stopping, and clear off.'

'OK.' Flint nodded. *Was that a twitch, the briefest hint of a smile around Dad's mouth? Could that heart of ice be melting?* He slammed the door. 'Thanks!' And ran across the road.

A red-and-gold version of the Arsenal strip. Cool. And a green strip with orange flashes. Nice. Very nice. Gathered on the ground, players listened as their coach explained. He had one foot on the ball and was waving his arms.

Flint recognized a face from the village green games. It was Marcus; his eyebrows jumped in surprise. He nudged the boy next to him. Josh lifted his head, grinned and pointed.

The coach turned. 'You must be Flint.'

Flint nodded. Someone had clearly done some talking about him . . .

'You've already met most of my squad.'

The coach gestured. 'I understand you have talent.'

Flint felt himself blush.

The coach smiled. 'You're not from the village?'

'The village?'

'Upper Beckton,' explained the coach. 'The locals like to pretend it's rural.'

'No.' Flint smiled. 'I'm not.' *What was that suburb he and Dad had driven through?* 'I live in . . . Thepstow.'

'Oh – not far, then.' The coach held out his hand. 'I'm Mr Russell. But everyone calls me Coach. Have you come for a trial?'

'I'm a bit out of practice,' said Flint, 'but I'd love a chance.' He looked down at his dirty work jeans. 'I'm afraid I haven't got any kit with me. Dad dropped me off. It was a bit last minute. I was helping fix the car.'

'I'd like to take a look at you straight away,' said Mr Russell. 'We were about to have a practice session – A team versus B. There's plenty of kit for you to borrow – some of the boots might be a bit ropy. Otherwise, if you prefer, you can come back another time with your own gear. Up to you.'

'I'll stay and do it now,' said Flint.

'Excellent,' said Mr Russell. 'Josh'll take you to the kit room and show you what we've got.' He turned to Josh. 'Let's try him in an away-shirt to start off with. Take a bit of time with the boots – we want the best fit possible.' He chuckled. 'Got to give the boy a chance! Come and join in when you've done.'

He'd felt very self-conscious at first. Josh, Marcus, Rich – most of the boys he knew from before – were playing in the club's red-and-gold first strip. He'd been pitted against them with the orange-and-greens. It had been very odd: the boys who previously he'd only ever seen on opposite sides, now playing together. And he was playing against all of them.

Mr Russell had started him in midfield, over on the left. That had put him opposite Rich and, a little further back, Marcus. He wasn't left-footed, but with Rich and the rest of the A team constantly on the attack, his work had all been defensive – so the position had suited him fine.

He hadn't stood still for a second. In terms of marking, tackling, getting into position and passing, Mr Russell had been given plenty of opportunities to see what he was made of. His self-consciousness had quickly vanished. He'd been too busy. And if Mr Russell *had* been paying him any special attention, he'd not been aware of it.

'You got in some great tackles,' Mr Russell had commented at half-time. 'Let's try you on the other side this half. See what you're like in a less defensive situation.' He'd asked him to play attacking midfielder, interacting with Rich as much as possible. Rich was striker.

Rich wasn't happy.

Flint had known from the look on Rich's face, when Mr Russell first turned to greet him, that he was less than pleased by his arrival at Beckton Leigh. A couple of times during the first half Rich had come close to losing his temper when he took the ball off him in good clean tackles. Now they were supposed to be cooperating with each other, Rich wasn't happy at all.

Rich had scored *three* goals in the second half. The first had been a solo effort, but Flint had set up the two that followed. There had been plenty of praise, and Rich's irritation was showing. Increasingly, he played selfish with the ball, losing possession when a pass would've kept options open.

This fact had not been lost on Mr Russell. But timely cries of 'Teamwork!' when Rich was on the ball, had so far been in vain.

'Josh!' Marcus tapped the ball wide and ran on.

With a clever back-foot flick, Josh outwitted his marker, sprinted into open space and looked around for options.

Flint raised a hand and darted forward. Josh's pass came straight to his feet. He turned towards the goal and put on pace. B team defenders fell back to block his path. He belted the ball across to Rich and charged forward looking for gaps.

To Flint's surprise, Rich gave it back immediately. The timing couldn't have been worse: two defenders piled in straight away, hacking and shoving for all they were worth.

Flint turned. And turned again. Keeping the ball tightly controlled, he hung on to it.

'Flint!' Rich was suddenly round in front of him. 'Pass it out!'

Flint pushed the ball clear.

Rich twisted and sliced. The ball arched round the keeper's outstretched arms.

'Yeeees!' Rich punched the air and leapt.

But the ball was flying back off the post.

Flint lurched, side-stepped the keeper, and *dived*. The net shook. The whistle blew.

'Nice reflexes!' Josh offered a hand.

Mr Russell blew the whistle again. 'That's it, lads. Over. Shower time. Thank you all for your hard work.' He threw Flint a wink. 'Very out of practice, eh?'

Flint shrugged. 'I've got a lot of work to do, but I'm sure I'd pick up, practising regularly with a team.'

Mr Russell chuckled. 'Listen to him! If all my boys could play so well . . . out of practice . . .' He patted Flint on the back. 'Go and take a shower with your team-mates.'

'Does that mean I'm *in*?' gasped Flint.

Mr Russell smiled. 'You did *want* to join?'

Flint nodded. 'Of course.'

'Then, yes,' said Mr Russell. 'You are *in*.'

CHAPTER 7
SMELLS LIKE TEAM SPIRIT

One and in! He could scarcely believe it –
a single trial-cum-practice-session, and
now he was playing for the team! Flint
smiled to himself as he laced the borrowed
boots. Just like that. A midfielder for
Beckton Leigh in their fourth-round home
Cup-tie.

'Did you find a pair?' Josh poked his
head round the kit-room door.

'Yeah.' Flint nodded. 'I've got the same
ones I wore before.'

'They fit all right?'

'Could be better.'

The smell of rotten cabbage was more of
a problem. 'My dad's supposed to be taking
me to get some.' Flint spoke quickly,

68

ashamed of the lie. 'But he's been too busy.'

'As long as they're comfortable enough to play in. Nobody minds you borrowing boots from here. It's all old kit people have finished with, stuff that's not wanted any more.'

Flint stared at the scuffed, baggy leather. 'I used to have a really good pair.'

Josh picked up a boot from the box. Its partner dangled from the other end of the laces. 'There's nothing wrong with them. Boots get chucked because feet are too big. These used to be mine.' He dropped them back. 'They fit, that's the main thing. Ready?'

Flint nodded and sprang to his feet.

'I want to show you something.' Josh beckoned. 'Come and have a quick look.' He led Flint into a plush, carpeted room. Bar at one end. Large glass cabinet, pride of place, opposite. 'This is the club room, where all the socials take place. Careful you don't get mud on the carpet.'

Flint followed him to the cabinet. They examined the silverware.

'You might get your name on one of these.' Josh grinned. 'They're all the club's own awards – Top Goal Scorer, that sort of stuff. Beckton haven't actually won

69

anything as a club. Not for years.'

'Oi!' Marcus tapped on the window. 'Coach wants everyone in the changing room. Now.'

'OK.'

The boys hurried after him, their studs clattering on the concrete.

Instead of the excited pre-match buzz of ten minutes earlier, the changing room was hushed, tense.

'Good.' Mr Russell rose from his bench as Josh and Flint entered. 'That's us all here.' He clapped his hands together. 'Now – a pressing issue that must first be dealt with.' His head turned slowly, surveying the attentive faces. 'An unpleasant matter. At some time either before, during, or immediately after the last practice session, Justin Parker's wallet went missing.'

Mr Russell began pacing. 'There's no evidence it was theft, or that the wallet disappeared here on club premises. But if anybody has any light to shed on the matter, please do so – in private and in confidence. I'd hate for anything to destroy the morale which all of us are working so hard to build.'

Reaching the end of the room, Mr Russell turned. 'Morale is crucial to a team.' Lifting his head, he inhaled slowly and steadily through quivering nostrils. 'What's that I smell?'

Flint glanced at his boots.

Mr Russell sniffed and paced . . . sniffed and paced . . . looking from face to face. 'Mmmmm . . .' Boys began smiling. Slowly, a smile stretched Mr Russell's lips, too. 'Mmmmm . . . smells like *team spirit*.'

Suddenly, the boys were on their feet, chanting in one voice: '*Beckton Leigh, Beckton Leigh, Beckton Leigh . . .*'

Hammer Town were a fearsome-looking bunch. Their plain dark strip – blue shirts, blue shorts, blue socks, emphasized a stark blockiness. They were a hard-as-nails, inner-city side and they were going to knock Beckton Leigh right out of the Cup – or so their vocal supporters had been insisting in chants and songs since well before kick-off.

In spite of the drama of the first half, Beckton's supporters had proved far more restrained. There was, nevertheless, quite a crowd of them. Parents, sisters, brothers, uncles and aunts, friends – even grand-parents had turned up. Each player had a small group rooting for him, cheering and calling encouragement whenever he got involved in the action.

Not Flint. He didn't mind though. He had known what it felt like to have someone urging him on to glory . . . and would never forget. But he was happy to be able to keep his head down and concentrate on doing a good job.

There'd been plenty to be getting on with. The Hammers were not as superior as their supporters wanted to believe, but they'd kept up the pressure throughout the first half. Beckton, captained by Rich, had rarely got off the back foot. But they hadn't caved in either. The 2–2 scoreline at half-time had belied the monumental efforts made by both sides.

In the half-time dressing-room pep talk, Mr Russell had urged his midfield to push forward. 'When we get back out there, I want you going *all out*, looking for goals. Push it through to Rich. Get up there yourselves. Whatever it takes. If we can pop one in early, that'll take the wind out of their sails.'

Flint had taken him at his word. In the last few minutes alone he'd managed three shots on goal. The Hammers were defending well, but only the keeper had stopped the last.

It was a corner.

Rich headed over with the ball, scowling. 'Don't go getting any fancy ideas about stealing my glory, lightweight.' There was menace in his voice. 'Feed me the balls, and set up shots – then you might stick around.'

He came right up close. 'You're taking this one.' He slammed the ball hard into Flint's stomach. 'Nice and high, dropping for the far post. I'll be running in.'

Marcus was in the crowded goal mouth with Chris and André and half a dozen Hammers. Rich hurried towards the far side, watched keenly by his marker.

Flint measured his strides back from the ball and took a slow, steadying breath. *When had he last taken a corner?* Too long ago.

He ran. As his foot made contact, he knew it was good. The ball climbed as it crossed. Players jumped in procession, but the ball remained tantalizingly out of reach. Flint chased in.

Rich was running. The ball dropped, perfect for him, just in front of the far post. He dived.

Hurling himself sideways, the giant keeper stretched a finger to the ball.

73

As Rich and the keeper collided, Flint tore into the six-yard box. The ball was still floating in the goal mouth.

Defenders flailed and dived. Attackers pushed and collided. Somewhere in the midst of the mad scramble, a falling Hammer volleyed from the line.

Flint flung himself, head first, at the outcoming missile. The ball cannoned straight back on target. And this time there was no-one to block.

Throwing his head back, Flint laughed out loud. His breath made golden clouds under the street lamp.

The darkness swallowed his laughter. River and night.

It was crazy: nearly home and still he couldn't stop grinning. He felt ridiculous. He'd been doing it the whole way, alone in the cold dark, grinning and chuckling like a complete nutter. It felt good to let it out. He'd forgotten what a thrill it could be – scoring in front of a crowd. What a *buzz*.

And to do it in *borrowed* boots – a new thrill altogether! The boots weren't so bad. Josh had told him to take them home and look after them. Keep them. They'd belonged to a boy who'd left the club.

Freshen 'em up and he'd have an OK pair of his own.

Flint bent and massaged his knee. He had run or jogged all the way from the club. After such a tough game, it was outrageous. He didn't even feel tired. Such a great feeling shouldn't be allowed.

Leaning against the railing, he stared out into the glassy, liquid darkness. *'Yeeeees!'* he yelled. *'Beauuuuutiful!'*

What was that? Flint jerked round. Back along the path, in the shadows beyond the last street lamp, something made a sharp, snapping sound. Like a foot stepping on a brittle twig.

Someone was back there.

Watching him.

Listening.

Lurking.

CHAPTER 8
TROUBLE

Flint squinted, but it was pointless. The light was dazzling. If there was someone back there, back down the path, it was impossible to see.

He turned away to face the river again. Not laughing this time, or yelling. Closing his eyes, he held his breath. If there was someone there, they had heard his shouts and laughter. He listened.

What could he hear? The hushed roar of the distant weir, down past the marina. A plane. A car. Cars. A horn sounding. Some deeper, far-off rhythm – a train maybe – or some kind of factory noise, carried on the night air?

The river, in spite of its vast size, slid past

in awesome silence. Only the occasional lap or gurgle gave away its presence.

Someone was there. He could sense them. There was no particular sound; more an absence – like a hole, or a shadow. In the dark beyond the street lights.

Flint shivered. That heat, and that good, good feeling he'd generated were dwindling fast. He turned towards home and set off at a brisk pace.

He could no longer see his breath. He had passed the scrapyard, passed the big bare backs of the warehouse buildings. He was in total darkness now. Last stretch before home. The illuminated sign of the marina shop flickered in the distance.

He glanced back. A shape moved into the shadows cast by the final street lamp. Someone *was* following him.

He quickened his pace. *Who might it be? Why would anybody take the trouble?* If he acted fast, he could use the dark. His eyes were adjusting to it. He knew this stretch of path. There were places he could hide.

Hurrying, he stumbled on the rough ground. The night had grown colder. He was shivering.

He peered into the darkness ahead, struggling to match vague shapes to what he could remember from the daylight. What was there along this stretch he could use as cover? The night was so black away from the street lamps, he might crouch beside the path and not be seen.

Below the ghosts of derelict houses an overgrown bank sloped down to the path. It was ugly in the daylight, with rubble and rubbish strewn amongst the trees. About halfway along there was an old concrete bunker which was large enough to hide behind.

Spotting the shape ahead, Flint scrambled off the path. He stepped carefully, creeping his way, then crouched against a rough wall. Low electric buzzing came from inside.

He was shaking, shivering with cold and – *what was it*?

Fear.

Footsteps were coming. A brisk *crunch-crunch* on the gravel. They stopped.

He peered. *Was that a shape?* He held his breath.

A sniff. A shudder of breath. *Crunch-crunch*. Footsteps again.

Something was moving along the path.

He slid a foot away from the wall, shifted his weight, gliding, through darkness and rubble, onto the path.

The silhouette was just a couple of metres in front.

Crack. Too late he felt the twig snap beneath his trainer.

Feet swivelled on the gravel ahead. *Crunch-crunch-crunch . . .*

The darkness hit him full on, in the chest, lifting him off his feet. It carried him backwards, into the ground.

It was on top of him, crushing him. It had hands. Arms. It was clutching his shoulder, pushing against his chin.

He grabbed, yanked, rolled. Bracing arm against neck, he dug his knees hard into the body beneath him.

'*Aaagh!*' The body writhed and lashed out.

Flint grappled the free arm.

'You scum-bag!'

Flint froze. 'Rich?' Staring hard, he could just about make out the features. *Was it?*

The body shoved hard, trying to topple him sideways. 'Get *off* me!'

Flint allowed himself to be pushed clear.

'Get off me, you dirty little *tramp.*' Rich. Unmistakably.

Flint peered at the sprawled figure. 'What are *you* doing here?'

Rich scrambled to his feet.

Flint did the same. 'What d'you want? Why did you attack me?'

'Attack *you*!' Rich spat the words. 'Who crept up on who? You're lucky I didn't *kill* you.'

'You've been following me,' said Flint.

'I *don't* think so!' Rich's tone was sneering. 'This is a public footpath. I'm *allowed* to walk along it.'

'Yeah, right.' Flint fought off a shiver. 'Look – you've made it very plain, more than once, that you don't like me . . .'

'But that didn't put you off – showing up where you're not wanted.'

'The club, you mean? You're not the club . . .'

'Aren't I?' Rich snorted. 'D'you know who my father is? He practically owns Beckton – the village, the golf club *and* the YFC. Beckton Leigh is just one of his little hobbies. What's your father? Some kind of tramp, judging by the way you dress. Probably a thief too.' Rich chuckled. 'Like father, like son.'

Flint forced himself to take slow deep breaths. 'Anything else you've got to say?'

Rich's laughter floated in the dark.

'OK.' Flint stepped past, back onto the path. 'I'm off.'

'Back home to your caravan?'

Flint turned. '*What?*'

'That's all there is down this way. Some grotty old site, full of clapped-out caravans. Are you going to your trailer-park?'

Flint felt himself tensing. 'What you on about?'

'Or d'you live on a boat?'

'No.'

'You lied,' said Rich. 'Every time anyone's asked you questions – about who you are, or where you live – you've *lied*. I know when someone's lying. I can tell.' He took a step closer. 'You said you lived in Thepstow. I know Thepstow boys from school. It's quite nice, actually, as neighbourhoods go. But you jogged past it fifteen minutes ago.'

'Your point being?'

'You're a liar,' said Rich, 'and *you've got something to hide.*'

'He's the team captain,' said Flint. 'Not exactly a friend, though.'

'You don't get on?' Saff followed him through to the boat's living room.

'He doesn't like me. Don't ask me why.' Flint shrugged. 'When I first met up with this lot, I lied about where I lived.'

'You thought they might reject you?'

'I dunno. Perhaps . . .' Flint shook his head. 'No, I lied because of Dad. He's always told me not to let people know where we live.' He picked mud from a fingernail. 'I suppose I wasn't keen to reveal too much either. But it was all right. Nobody really asked much after that.'

He plonked down on the cushioned bench. 'But Rich is a different matter. He followed me, spying on me to find out where I live. He wants me out of the club.'

'Why?'

'I don't think he likes having competition. He's been top-dog for a long while. I've got in the odd tackle, and now he's got the hump.'

'You think now that he knows where you live, he'll use it somehow against you?'

Flint shrugged. 'I told him I was only visiting a friend. I told him he'd got it all wrong and made out I was on my way round here. But I don't think he believed me.'

Saff shook her head.

'Sorry,' said Flint. 'Things get a bit tricky living with Dad.'

'I'm sure.' Saff chuckled. 'I don't know how you manage.'

Flint grunted. 'I don't have any choice.'

'You staying for a cup of tea?' Saff's head poked back through the bead curtain.

Flint nodded.

'Hang on a minute – wasn't today your first game with the new club?'

'That's right. A Cup match.'

Saff's face lit up. 'Well, don't keep me in suspenders! How did you get on?'

'We won.'

Saff gave a loud whoop.

'Beckton Leigh go through to the next round.'

'Brilliant!' said Saff. 'And what about you? Any good shots, tackles, passes? How d'you think you played?'

Flint smiled. Such a contrast to Dad. Mum had always had the same enthusiasm, been eager to find out how he'd done. 'I scored.'

'You *scored!*' Saff grabbed him. 'Your first game!' She was shaking him. 'That's fantastic!'

Flint laughed.

'Oh, that's wonderful!' Saff looked so pleased for him. She practically had tears in her eyes. 'So you think you played well?'

'Yeah. On the whole.'

Saff tutted. 'So modest.' She shook her head and plunged back through the bead curtain, laughing. 'Your dad was the same.'

'Dad?' Flint followed her through into the kitchen. 'How d'you mean?'

'When *he* scored . . .' Saff froze. 'Oh God . . .' She turned to look at him. 'I've put my foot in it, haven't I?'

'Scored?' Flint slumped against the work-top. 'Dad?'

'He hasn't told you, has he?'

CHAPTER 9
TAKING SIDES

It was freezing. The ground, the grass, the trees, everything was dusted with frost. The grey sky had a pale, washed-out look. The river was dark and glassy.

Flint switched from a jog to sideways skips – it looked pretty silly, no doubt, but was a good little stretch for the hips. Living so far from his friends was a pain, but at least it gave him the opportunity for an all-round warm-up. Most never bothered.

Stitch. He gasped and clutched the pain. Time for a touch of dawdling. He'd done enough, some days his heart wasn't really in it.

He felt rough. Badly. Dad had been asleep when he'd got in, still snoring when he'd got up. *And* when he left. It'd been a mad restless night, after the chat round at Saff's. It was still hard to take in what she'd told him.

Dad – his dad, the Dad that Mum hated so much she never talked about him . . . the Dad *he* hated . . . the Dad who, till very recently, had been guaranteed to turn very nasty at even a passing reference to the game . . . he'd once been a professional footballer! Unbelievable.

Dad had played for the national Under 21's. He'd spent nearly two years with United. Been popular too – a rising young star, Saff had said, before injury took him out for good. The injury that still plagued him, all these years later. And the bitter disappointment. He must have been gutted. It explained a lot. Well, *some* things.

Flint stopped and stared. The village green was a scene from a Christmas card. White, and eerily still. A matchstick man's dog barked in the distance. Frosted roofs, trees and church spire. Pretty.

He hacked the ground with his heel. Rock hard. It'd be lethal to play on.

Saff was convinced that Dad was, at last, changing his ways. His recent promises and 'changes in attitude' were evidence in her eyes. She was so hopeful. But she'd warned: if Dad found out what the two of them had discussed, things could turn very sour.

She was going away for a while to do some painting work on a boat moored on the coast. She'd miss the quarter-finals. Nor would she be back in time for the semis, or the final – supposing Beckton did that well. But she had made him a promise, too. There'd still be league games – she'd come and watch Beckton as soon as she got back. She'd said she'd try and persuade Dad to come, too. She was a dreamer.

Flint tried a gentle jog. The stitch had eased – it was almost comfortable. Increasing his pace, he crossed the village green: cruising speed, enjoying the chill air . . . and the peace.

At the far end, the village nestled round the church – a large pub and clusters of houses. Several of the Beckton boys lived here.

Spotting Josh's gate, Flint sprinted.

The porch door opened. Josh grinned. 'Nice surprise.'

'I thought I'd call and see if you were ready.' Gingerly climbing icy steps, Flint stamped his feet on the doormat. 'I woke early.'

'Come in.' Josh pushed open the inner door.

'It's all right.' Flint held back. 'I'll wait here.'

'Don't be silly.'

'Nah.' Flint pointed to his frost-covered trainers. 'I'll wait in the porch. We can have a warm-up if you get a move on.'

'OK. I won't be a sec.' Josh disappeared through one of the doors off the hall.

Flint felt uneasy. Recently, he'd only been in people's houses at the dead of night.

The hall was wide, with cornices, a high white ceiling and central staircase. Soft peachy walls were hung with mirrors and paintings. Flint tested the carpet with his foot. Luxurious thickness. Polished wooden tables stood on either side of the stairs, each carrying a shiny black statuette. Tasteful. Classy, even. *Expensive*.

'Out of my way.' Rich barged sideways.

Flint flailed his arms in an effort to keep his balance on the slippery ground.

Recovering his grip, he gave chase.

Three defenders were blocking Rich's path. André signalled for the ball to his left, but instead he cut right, heading for the open wing.

Flint accelerated, easily matching Rich's pace. Rich's arms pumped like pistons. He grunted, glancing over his shoulder.

Flint leapt. 'Gotcha!' In one swift sliding move, he sliced the ball out from under Rich's legs, hit the hard ground and went bum-surfing towards the road.

'Tackled!' yelled Josh.

'Excellent!'

Flint scrambled to his feet and recovered the ball.

'Dirty, fouling toe-rag!' Rich was coming, snarling. 'Just what I'd expect from a scrounger.'

Scrounger? Flint danced the ball from foot to foot. Rich closed. Flint twisted right, ducked and lurched left. Suddenly, as his legs began to churn, his shirt tightened around his neck, gagging him, pulling him back . . .

'I'll give you *gotcha!*' Rich's voice hissed close to his ear.

Flint reached for his collar, jack-knifed.

'*Aagh!*'

As he tumbled, his hip smashed against something softer. Rich writhed beneath him, grunting and clutching himself.

Flint got to his feet. The ball was trickling towards the road. Standing over Rich, he held out a hand.

Rich glared up at him, sucking breath through clenched teeth. His eyes filled with hate, suddenly he laughed. 'Got to you, didn't I?' He pushed the hand away and spat. 'Back off, you lying, caravan park tramp. Or do you want your new friends to find out where you really live?'

Flint stared as Rich staggered to his feet and jogged after the ball.

'Come on, Flint!'

Flint turned. The other players stood watching. Josh was pointing.

Rich had retrieved the ball. He began to run with it, to pick up pace. Watching him approach, Flint tried to side-step to block his path, but his legs felt leaden.

Rich bared his teeth. '*Back off!*' he growled and shot past.

'Flint! *Tackle* him! What are you doing!'

Flint stumbled.

Ploughing past first Josh and then Marcus, Rich rounded the remaining defenders, skipped, swerved, and blasted the ball between the posts.

Dad was sitting in the dark, watching the portable. The gas fire glowed. The gloom was toasty, streaked thick with cigarette fug.

Swallowing a last gulp of air, Flint pulled the door closed.

Dad nodded. 'How d'you get on?'

Flint peered past the empty bottle. *What did he see – a broken man? A man struggling with disappointment?* 'Not great.'

Dad grunted, gazing into the screen.

In his tiny room Flint kicked off the trainers, slipped out of damp jeans and ferreted for a dry pair.

Dad's deep belly-laugh drowned out the TV. It dissolved into coughing. 'Flint . . .' He coughed to clear his throat. 'Flint – your little mate . . . Richard?'

'My team captain . . . he's not exactly a *mate*.'

'What's his surname – something *poncey*?' Dad chuckled. 'Lampton-Planet?'

'Langston-Prannett.' Flint felt his skin prickle. 'Why?'

Dad grunted. 'What's their place like?'

'Beechcroft? Absolutely massive – a mansion. Why?'

'Any chance you'd get invited?'

'*What?*'

Dad appeared in the doorway. 'I need you to have a look round.'

'What!' Flint stared.

Dad's mouth made a dry sucking noise. 'Mr Langston-Prannett owns a valuable painting.' The eyes widened. '*Very.*'

'Painting?' Flint pulled on his jeans. 'A *painting?*' His voice croaked. 'Why would you be interested in a painting?'

The hollow stare.

'But what about . . . ? You *promised* Saff.'

Dad shook his head. 'No TVs and videos – that's all the promise was. This is different. A *to order* job.'

'But . . .' Flint stammered, 'Rich *hates* me.'

'Hates you?' Dad frowned. A sneer, trying to be a smile, slowly spread across his face. He chuckled. 'Nothing else for it then . . .'

CHAPTER 10

BEECHCROFT

'What if someone wakes?'

'They won't, if you do it right.' Dad flicked his lighter and cupped his big, rock-steady hands to a cigarette. The flame died into darkness.

It was freezing. 'I'm nervous.' Flint clenched and relaxed his muscles, but it didn't stop the shaking. He struggled with the gloves. 'What if I screw up?'

'You won't. You never have.'

'I've never done a house where people know me.'

'It's no different.'

'What if things go wrong?'

'They won't.'

The cigarette end glowed.

93

'What if I get caught?'

'Know your exit routes.' Dad exhaled, long and slow. 'Then you won't.'

'But what if I do . . . ?'

'Don't.' The dial lit up on Dad's watch. Leaning across, he opened Flint's door. 'Time to go.'

Flint fitted the backpack. 'You *will* be here?'

Dad nodded. 'You're forgetting something.' He reached the balaclava from the dash, and chucked it over. 'Keep it on.'

With a sigh, Flint pulled the balaclava over his head. He hated it – the itchy material, the sinister feel. Giving a mock salute, he closed the door and headed off down the street.

At the darkest point between two street lamps he cut towards the wall. *Where was it?* Brushing his hands back and forth across the rough brickwork, he felt with gloved fingertips. Somewhere there was a six-inch nail jammed into the crumbling mortar at about waist height.

Found it! He gave a sharp yank to check it was still secure. Then, placing his foot, he reached and pushed up. Directly above, fumbling fingers caught the hoped-for hold. His second foot-hold, nail number two, was where it should be. It was just a scramble to the top of the wall.

The pickup kicked into life. Flint watched it chug down the empty street. It pulled into the main road, the rear lights flashed. Then it was gone.

Wind gusted. Four metres, a leap into darkness. And this – just to *get to* the house. Flint eased himself over the edge, gripping the wall with his trainers. Only when he'd lowered himself as far as he could, did he push away and let go.

He rolled. Nothing broken by the drop. What next? *Know your exit routes*. Check the gate. He picked himself up.

Staying close to the wall, he jogged round to the front of the house. The garden was huge. Still no stars or moon above, and no sign of things changing – that was good. Cloud was an ally.

Ahead, the large, floodlit gate stood out against the darkness. A camera's infrared eye glinted from its perch. He was probably already being recorded. There was no time to hang about.

His breath smoked in the light. Keeping his head low, he moved swiftly to a single black button at the side of the gate. The manual lock release. It'd be nice to have the luxury of testing it. But too risky. There might be some kind of signal or alarm. The clunk of the lock releasing the big iron gates could be enough to wake someone. Knowing the button was there would have to be enough.

He ran silently towards the house, creeping low across the lawns, round the side to the double garage. Up the low wall, then a jump and scramble onto the tarred roof. For such a slight slope, the roof was surprisingly slippery. That meant frost. Frost was bad news. Frost was an enemy.

The garage roof stretched to the side of the house. Rough stonework provided the footholds up to a drainpipe. He tested it with his weight. Sound.

With a heave and a kick, Flint hooked a foot over the pipe, then reached for the sill. Blood thundered in his ears. He reached again. Nearly there. One more try.

Got it! Home and dry. Well, almost.

Hoisting himself up, onto the ledge, he leant against the glass and panted. Moment of truth time. Fingers against the wooden frame, firm pressure upwards. He pushed, muffling a grunt.

Nothing.

He took a long deep breath. Now what?

His head wasn't good for heights, even in the dark. Dad had been certain the window would open. If it didn't, plans were scuppered. Try again. Count to three. And *puuuuuush!*

Nothing.

Calm head. This wasn't funny – wasn't funny at all. He held the laugh down. Nerves. It was fear . . . panic. Slow breathing would help, but the lungs were chasing a racing heart. One more try. Deep breath . . . *three, and . . .*

Wummmp!

He tumbled, shielding his head with his arms. Darkness span. Softness cushioned the heavy fall. He lay deathly still on thick carpet, listening.

The silence of a soundly sleeping house. Ticking clocks, wind-rattled windows, snores and heavy breathing.

Time to get searching.

Creeping his way along the landing, he checked behind each open door. Bathroom . . . bedroom, snoring, two adults sleeping . . . bedroom, young girl and teddies, silently sleeping . . . bedroom, boy, teddy . . . *Hang on!* Flint stopped in his tracks and turned back. He had almost missed it in the dark. That was *Rich* – on his back, with his mouth open, looking grosser even than normal. And, tucked under sleeping beauty's arm . . . a *teddy*!

Rich made a long-drawn-out snuffling sound. He snorted, mumbled and tossed his head. Clutching the teddy tighter, he settled on his side and began to snore. The snores grew louder.

Flint pulled himself away. Laughter was in danger of returning. He still had work to be getting on with.

Time for the torch.

Carefully testing each step for creaks, he made his way down the wide staircase – with room for three or more abreast, it was a grand affair – hugging first one wall, then another, before thrusting into the vast hall.

The beam showed framed paintings all the way down, and more in the hall. But first things first. *Know your exit routes.* Flint hurried down the stairs and crossed the hall to the front door: two heavy bolts, a latch and a mortice. He turned the key till the mortice clicked, slid back the bolts and twisted the latch.

A freezing gust stung his eyes. He peered: grainy darkness, stuff swirling. *Snow.* Snow was falling! His heart leapt, and *sank*. A momentary thrill, crushed. Tonight, of all nights, snow was one thing he didn't need. Now he'd really have to *hurry*. If it settled, there'd be footprints. Big trouble.

There was no time now to look for back-up exit routes. He had to find the painting fast. All doors into the hall were closed . . . and locked. Flint reached into his bag for the fluted security-lock key. Designed to prevent access to the main hall for anyone coming in through a downstairs window, the locks were no deterrent against an intruder already on the inside.

Choosing the nearest door, Flint opened it and probed with the torch-beam. Two enormous sofas . . . several armchairs . . . a television. There were pictures on the walls. He moved closer to take a look. Photographs. Huge family portraits. The torch bounced off a much larger framed picture across the room. A full-length, painted portrait of a woman in big billowy skirts and a powdered wig. Impressive. But not what he was after.

Moving across the hall, he tried the door opposite. The dining room. An elegant oval table, eight chairs, and – the torch-beam shone back in his face – something big in a frame. No use to him, whatever it was.

Fronted by glass, there'd be no way to cut it from the frame without taking the whole thing off the wall. That was not a job for one person.

Flint stopped and stared. A lone sailor . . . a battered sailing boat . . . a stormy sea . . . The painting itself should be stormy, Dad had said; kind of wild and messy-looking. *Bingo*. Wouldn't you just know it! Here it was, right in front of him. Protected by glass. *Now what was he supposed to do?*

Propping the torch on the table, he slumped into a chair and gazed at the painting in front of him. Dad was mad – and *he* was even crazier to be here. He should have run away. He should have done it long ago. He should never have allowed this to happen.

It was a demonic sea. The waves around the boat seemed to arch right into the sky, forming a swirling frame round the stricken boat. The single mast had been snapped. Lashed by wind and sea, a sailor in oilskins clutched the wheel. He stared up, out of the chaos, out of the picture, blazing defiance. For a strange moment Flint had the sensation *he* was falling, falling *in*, spiralling down inside the waves, to stand on the deck.

He shuddered and stepped closer to examine the small plaque at the bottom. Scrolly, antique letters: *A Certain Kind of Courage*.

What was that? Clicking off the torch, Flint span round.

A sound – coming from the hall. He hurried to the door and peered through the crack. Still dazzled from the torch, his eyes struggled. He blinked. The main part of the staircase was directly above and hidden from view. Slow and rhythmical, with a steady tread, *someone* was coming down.

Slipping out into the hall, Flint pulled the door shut. He pressed himself against the wall and slowly crept along to where he could see the stairs. He peered: a pale figure, standing, motionless, halfway down. He dropped and fought to slow his breath.

A sound. His heart jumped. A voice! Something like a cry. *What was it?*

'You can't tell me what to do.' A girl's soft voice, scarcely more than a whisper.

Flint felt his body try to squeeze itself small.

'I don't have to do what you say.'

Slowly lifting himself, he craned and peered. The white shape hadn't moved. It had pale arms and legs, a girl's face, frowning. The eyes were *open*. They stared.

Rich's sister – from the family photos. Flint watched; watched and shivered. It was freezing. The motionless girl wore only a nightie. *Was she sleep-walking?*

'Sticks and stones . . .' said the girl; 'you can't make me.' She turned and, with slow, measured steps, began climbing the stairs.

Flint pulled himself upright and backed towards the front door. Time to leave. The girl was nearing the top of the stairs.

He turned the latch and tugged. An icy gust pushed against the door and squeezed past him, chilling him to the bone. He stared in horror.

The cloud had cleared. A shiny moon hung in the sky. Where before there'd been lawns and a driveway leading to the gate, now there was a blanket of glowing white.

Snow.

Flint pulled the sleeping-bag up round his shoulders. It wouldn't stop the shivering, he knew that.

'Get this down you.' Dad put a steaming

102

mug on the table in front of him. 'You'll soon be warm.'

It wasn't just the cold that was making him shiver. It was *fear*. *Loads* of it. So much, it was hard to begin unravelling. His stomach was a knot. He sipped. Hot and sweet. A tea-bag bobbed at the surface.

'Don't worry.' Dad plonked down opposite. Topping up his own mug from the bottle, he slurped. 'The two of us together'll be able to manage it.' He tapped the side of his head. 'Brains here'll think of a way.'

Flint nodded. He didn't want to manage it. He didn't want that. He didn't want any more of this life – Dad and his mad, bad schemes. He'd never wanted it. He'd had enough. Long ago.

Wind buffeted the caravan. Dad chinked the bottle against his mug. The smell of whisky drifted across the table.

Flint breathed warm moisture from the tea. Listening to Saff he'd been tempted into believing that something might change. But it wouldn't, and it was never going to. Dad cared about no-one but himself. Dad would never give him a normal, secure life. Dad would never be a parent he could trust, and not fear. *Was that really too much to ask?*

'Yes –' Dad was scariest when he spoke softly – 'in answer to what you were thinking.' He smiled. 'Yes, you *are* going to be all right. No-one's going to notice someone's been in the mansion.' He slurped. 'You left the window open, you left a couple of doors unlocked – that's nothing they won't explain away as forgetfulness.'

Flint shivered. 'But the footprints . . .'

'You used your initiative!' Dad chuckled. 'Breaking off a branch . . . sweeping as you went – where d'you learn that? I'm impressed!'

'There'll still be tracks. And anyway, I probably missed some – it was dark. They only have to check the video camera and they'll see me.'

'Half the time those things are just for show, they're not even connected to anything. When they are, more often than not there's no tape running.' Dad laughed. 'You were wearing your balaclava. Nobody's going to recognize you.'

Funny – he didn't feel reassured.

CHAPTER 11
AWAY

Overnight, the weather had turned to driving, icy sleet. As Flint jogged his way past the green, he noted with weary relief that not a trace of snow was left on the ground.

Shivering, he clambered up the coach steps. It was noisy and warm. Most of the team appeared to be already on board. Rich was sitting in the middle of the back row, with André, Nicholas and the rest of his mates, laughing and shouting.

Two rows in front, across the aisle from Marcus, Josh waved. 'I've saved you a seat.'

Rich's expression hardened; his grudging eyes followed Flint's approach. He nudged his companions and whispered.

Flint didn't need lip-reading skills to guess what was being said. He dropped into the seat next to Josh. 'What's Rich got against me?' he grunted.

'Haven't you worked it out yet?' Josh glanced back between the seats. 'He's a bullying loud-mouth. Not a bad striker, but useless as a captain. His father has a lot of clout at the club.'

Mr Russell progressed up the aisle, counting heads.

Flint frowned. 'So why does he pick on *me*?'

'You're showing him up for what he is.'

'I am?'

Josh smiled. 'You've got talent.'

'Right.' Mr Russell clapped his hands. 'Can I have quiet, please? I'm afraid, once again, I have distressing news before a match.' The coach fell silent. 'There has been a break-in.'

Gasps and whispers filled the coach. Flint gripped the seat. Felt his stomach knot. He was about to *die*.

'The club house has been burgled.'

'*No!*'

Flint grunted and dropped his face in his hands. Relief. 'That's terrible.'

'The trophy cabinet was raided and

three prize trophies – Goal-Scorer of the Year, Player of the Year and the Team Captain's Shield – have been stolen.'

'What!' Rich jumped up from his seat. 'The dirty, thieving—'

'*Thank* you, Richard!' Mr Russell raised a placating hand. 'You, of course, feel affronted, as current holder of all three trophies. The rest of us, I'm sure, share your feelings.' He looked from face to face. 'My concern, however, given the recent disappearance of a wallet, is the possibility of a link between these crimes – that they are being committed by a single individual, and that this may be someone associated with the club.'

Rich snorted. 'As if we didn't know who—'

'*Richard!*' Mr Russell scowled. 'That's *enough*. This is an extremely serious matter.'

An uncomfortable hush filled the coach. Flint stared at his feet.

'Investigations, of course, will have to be carried out,' said Mr Russell. 'If anybody has information they should come and talk to me. In the meantime, weather permitting, there's a match to be played, and a team to be beaten.'

*'Danvers three, Beckton nil, hal-le-luja!
Danvers three, Beckton nil, hal-le-lu-u-ja!'*
Danvers, in their mud-spattered grey,
were back out on the pitch, their
supporters in unrelentingly cheerful voice.

Flint shook his head. 'Every time I come
close to him, he's muttering stuff.'

'Don't let it get to you,' said Josh. 'He's
trying to mess you up.'

They followed their weary-looking teammates onto the pitch.

'It's not just Rich.' Flint groaned. It
was a nightmare: intermittent sleet, the
pitch a total bog – an *abysmal* first half.
Three goals down in the quarter-final!
Coach had been furious in the changing
room. The team were playing atrociously.
But *he* had played worst of all. The worst
game of his life.

'What then?' said Josh.

Flint booted a piece of churned-up turf.
'You're the only one who's passing to me.
Even Marcus – I can see it in his eyes – he
hesitates every time.'

Josh put a hand on his shoulder. 'You
have made some blunders.'

'I feel like no-one trusts me.'

Josh tapped his forehead. 'It's all in here.

You've got to show them. You've got to trust *yourself*. What Rich said in the bus was out of order. *I* know you wouldn't do a thing like that.'

'Do you?'

'Of course.' Josh smiled. 'So do most of them. But they need to see you're not fazed.'

'Not fazed!' gasped Flint. *Guilty conscience*. 'Rich has been dissing and slating and just generally saying things about me since day one. They think I stole the cups!'

'Don't worry about what they think.' Josh patted him on the back. 'You're *good*. Play your best.'

They jogged to their positions.

It was Danvers' kick-off. Moving the ball swiftly to the wing, they pushed forward.

André went in for the tackle, and lost. Nicholas followed suit. Suddenly, Beckton were once again in retreat, the midfield falling back in a desperate attempt to shore up their defence.

The ball curled in from the wing, straight to Danvers' dangerous striker. Ready and waiting, Josh met the player head-on. The two boys went down, but that didn't stop them struggling for possession.

There in a second, Flint hooked the ball free and took his bearings on the field. *Don't let it get to you.*

The Danvers forwards were homing in. Dodging and jumping tackles as he ran, Flint cut a swathe to the left wing. The ground was like thick chocolate cake-mix – lumpy mud, sucking on his boots with every step. *Play your best.*

Rich loitered in the middle, tightly marked. Marcus was way up the wing, running forward. Finding space, Flint lofted the ball. 'Marcus!'

Marcus glanced back, saw it, and adjusted to collect. Defenders ran out to intercept.

Flint pushed forward to back up his teammate. The ball came straight back.

'Go for it!' yelled Mr Russell.

Danvers' midfield were caught on the hop. Flint passed one, then another. And *another*. Entering the penalty area, he found defenders blocking his way. He passed the ball back out to Marcus. Ahead of him, Rich was still trying to shake his marker.

Pursued to the very edge of the goal-line, Marcus twisted sharply back and levered the ball high.

'Mine!' Rich leapt . . . too early. His marker jumped short.

Flint charged and dived, sliding through the mud. The net jerked in front of him.

'Goal!'

Yes! He had done it. The magic was back.

Marcus helped him to his feet. He felt lighter. Marcus was grinning. 'Nice work!'

Rich scowled. 'Yeah – lovely! Shame about the lousy pass.'

Marcus and Flint jogged back together.

'Come on, Beckton! Beckton – come on!' The supporters had finally found their voice.

Determined to regain momentum, Danvers were quick to take the kick. But, brimming with new confidence, Flint charged at the first pass. Catching everyone, himself included, by surprise, he deflected the ball.

'Go Flint, go!'

He took off, straight down the middle, into the opposition half, the sound of Josh's voice spurring him on. He pumped his legs; he needed unstoppable momentum. Rich was keeping up on his left. With perfect timing, Flint punted the ball to him and skipped a sliding tackle. He pushed forward, ready to receive back. 'Rich! On the inside. I can take it.'

Rich weaved round one, through two more. But the mud was slowing him. There were too many opposition players on his case. He stumbled. He staggered. As he fell, his hand went up for a foul. None had been committed – none was given.

Before the Danvers players could make use of possession, Flint was in their midst, stealing the ball back. He left in a hurry.

'Run with it!' yelled Josh from somewhere to the rear. 'I'm behind you. Let's take it *all the way*.'

Marcus was pushing forward on the left, André on the right.

'*Beck-ton!*' For the first time, Beckton's supporters were out-shouting the opposition's.

Flint darted, first left, then right; turning sharply, confidently, he threw the greys off balance, broke their stride, left them in the mud. He had brought the ball to the edge of the box, but *he* knew when it was time to pass. 'Josh!' With three defenders blocking his way, he dummied a side-swipe, then back-heeled.

Josh shot past with the ball. The Danvers defenders gave chase; Flint too.

Marcus and André closed in from the wings.

Josh tapped the ball to Marcus, and swerved round the remaining defender. Marcus staggered. It was an awkward ball. He volleyed on the run.

Flint was two metres behind Josh, and closing. The ball was flying over their heads. The keeper darted across his goal, following the ball, ready for the shot. But André was travelling too fast. As he braked to control the ball, his supporting leg slid from under him. Down he went, arms and legs flailing. The ball rolled.

'Yours!' yelled Josh, sliding through the mud towards the left post.

Flint whacked it, full force. The keeper went down like a nine-pin. But the ball was still in play!

Josh hacked, missed, collided – banging heads with a defender. The two boys toppled together.

Flint slipped, slithered and staggered.

The keeper was scrambling to his feet, looking for the ball. It was rolling away from the goal. Mud everywhere. A defender was charging in to clear.

Flint hurled himself, feet-first.

He felt his instep make contact. He felt

the sharp stab of pain as the defender's boot crunched into his thigh. He heard a cry of agony . . .

Darkness – a small window of sky, framed by shadowy faces; the ground cold and wet beneath him.

'How's he doing?'

'He's awfully pale.'

'How you feeling, son?'

He felt bad – *seriously* bad – cold, sick and giddy. His thigh was killing him. The faces seemed far off – he felt as if he'd shrunk deep down inside himself. He could hear funny groaning noises. They were coming from his own throat.

Mr Russell knelt. 'Stand back please, everybody. He needs to breathe.'

With a push from behind, Flint sat up. He puffed out his cheeks and slowly, gently, shook his head. He was on the touchline. 'How did I . . . what *happened*?'

'You scored another goal,' said Josh. '*That's* what!'

'You also got a kick in the leg.' A boy Flint didn't recognize stepped forward. He was wearing grey – what could be seen of it beneath the mud. One of the Danvers players. 'Sorry, mate. It was quite a hard one. I think you almost passed out.'

'Big nerve in the thigh,' said Mr Russell. 'It can do that sometimes, if you whack it hard enough. There doesn't appear to be anything broken, though. How's the leg feeling now?'

'It aches a touch.' Flint bent it and straightened it. 'I'll probably have a bruise.' Grabbing the hand offered by the Danvers boy, he tried to pull himself up.

'Whoa! Hang on a minute.' Mr Russell shook his head. 'You just rest where you are for a while.'

'I'd like to restart the game,' said the ref.

'No problem.' Mr Russell nodded. 'No substitutions at this stage. I'm sure he'll be fine.'

The ref gave the thumbs up. 'Seems pretty keen to get back.'

On the whistle, Danvers took their kick. Flint scrambled to his feet.

'Hold your horses!' Mr Russell grabbed his shoulders. 'Let me finish my checks – make sure everything's OK.'

Flint anxiously watched the pitch as Mr Russell rubbed and manipulated his leg. If Beckton lost the momentum now, they lost everything. He patted the thigh. 'I feel fine, Coach. Honest.'

115

Mr Russell smiled. 'You're fine when I say so. Give me ten star-jumps.'

Flint grunted.

Mr Russell pointed to the home goal-line. 'And a run to the end and back.'

Puffing in protest, Flint crouched . . . leapt and crouched . . . 'One!' . . . leapt and crouched . . . 'Two!' . . . leapt and crouched . . .

On the pitch the greys were advancing cautiously, passing and running, passing and running. Rich bellowed from the centre line. He was too far from the action.

'Ten!' Flint set off for the corner flag.

Danvers' danger-man had the ball. He loped gently towards the defenders, as he had done so many times in the first half, gathering speed, his forwards spread out on either side, stretching the defence.

'Go on, Josh. Take him!' Flint spurted towards the corner-post, willing his team-mate to act. He touched the flag and turned. Danger-man was down in the mud! Josh was swerving to avoid a tackle. 'Yes! Go on, mate!' Flint sprinted. 'Go on!'

Two of Danvers' midfield players pushed forward to cut Josh off. He passed to Marcus. The greys turned their attention to the wing.

'Force a deflection,' bellowed Mr Russell.

Leading his pursuers to the touchline, Marcus deftly carried out the order. The whistle blew for the throw-in.

Flint staggered to a halt.

'OK.' Mr Russell gave him the nod. 'Go get 'em.'

'Nice!' Flint patted Marcus on the back, slapped hands with Josh and ran towards the middle of the pitch.

Rich scowled as he approached. 'You're a midfielder, Flint, not a striker. Just remember that.'

Flint halted. 'You might be captain, but it's down to Coach to tell me my job. Try showing some leadership for a change.'

Rich came closer. 'D'you want everyone to know you live in a *caravan*?' He sneered as he spat the last word.

'Could be worse,' muttered Flint. 'At least I don't sleep with a teddy.'

'*What!*' Rich's face turned purple.

Flint bit his lip. That was stupid. Risky to have mentioned. 'I said, let's concentrate – get ready.' He winked. 'Shall we?'

Rich glowered.

A short blast on the whistle. Marcus took the throw . . . back to Josh . . . Flint found space and signalled . . . Josh pushed forward and passed.

117

Flint dallied – let Danvers sweat while his teammates moved forward. A midfielder advanced to confront. Flint dummied left, pushed the ball between tired legs, and cut right. Another grey closed in. *Where to?* Wide, to André.

André ran with the ball. Outstripping his marker, he gained twenty metres, then passed to Josh. Josh dribbled past two and chipped to Rich. Rich dithered. He looked back, confused.

'Go on!' yelled Flint. 'You've got support.'

The captain was galvanized. Bursting into the penalty area, he swerved and gathered speed. Flint chased him, gaining on him, Josh panting to the side.

Rich jumped a tackle, slipped, staggered, regained his balance. Two defenders blocked his path. He twisted, scooping the ball away as he tumbled.

'Yours!' Josh toe-poked it to Flint.

Flint swerved to collect, then darted towards the goal. The remaining greys raced to cut him off. Well-positioned, the keeper watched like a hawk. Dummying to Marcus on his left, Flint switched sharply right. Wrong-footed defenders flailed. He back-flicked, *high*.

The ball floated across the goal-mouth.

The keeper started to come out, then changed his mind and retreated. Too late! It clunked off the crossbar and *in*.

'*Yeeeees!*' Beckton's restrained supporters seemed suddenly overwhelmed by the excitement. As Flint and his team-mates jogged back to their own half, mums and dads burst into spontaneous chanting: '*Beckton Leigh, Beckton Leigh – one more goal!*'

Across the pitch, the Danvers supporters glowered.

On the touchline Mr Russell tapped his watch. 'Six minutes. Come on, lads, you can do it.'

Running in thick mud was exhausting and after nearly ninety minutes it was a miracle any player was left standing. But Danvers took their kick with one more burst of energy. The ball passed across and back; their forwards pushed up, ready to receive.

Flint's legs felt like lead. *Play your best*.

A poorly judged pass, and suddenly Flint was accelerating like a cheetah, racing Danvers' danger-man to the ball. They barged, collided, kept running, pushed one another. The striker grabbed Flint's shirt. Flint stretched for the ball, slammed on the brakes and hoofed it clear.

Unmarked on the wing, André collected, turned and ran.

'Get back!' yelled the Danvers coach. 'You're leaving yourselves wide open – cover the wing!'

Rich was heading into the penalty area. André had made such rapid ground, he was looking for someone to pass to.

Flint sprinted. It felt like a stampede, half the field running helter-skelter in the same direction.

'Come on, Beckton!' bellowed Mr Russell. 'You can do it, if you *hurry*.'

As the greys began closing André down, he changed direction and lofted the ball. There was a mad scramble for the wing. Marcus got there first and slipped the ball back to Josh.

Flint was inside the penalty area; Rich, on the six-yard line. Josh began a run. Dodging one, then another, he skipped and dodged his way past four of the opposition, before chipping the ball to Flint.

Barged and kicked, Flint knew this wasn't the moment to appeal. Keeping his harassers at bay, he signalled for help.

Josh swept past. 'One-two!'

Flint chipped.

'Come *on!*' yelled Mr Russell.

Flint side-stepped and collected. Rich was jostling defenders in the six-yard box. Pass or shoot – there wasn't time to think. He whacked it.

The net shook. Whistle blasts sealed the result.

'You were brilliant.' Josh patted Flint on the back. 'What a transformation!'

Flint smiled. 'We were a team.'

'You've brought the side to life.'

'Uh-uh.' Flint shook his head. 'Other way round.'

CHAPTER 12
SCRAP

Perhaps things *were* changing, after all . . .

Flint fiddled with pieces of broken wind-shield. Doggie eyes and ears lifted expectantly, alerted by the movement of his arm. 'Sorry, girls.' He showed his empty hands. 'No ball.'

Things weren't changing in the way Saff had hoped. Everything Dad did, he did for himself. He had made an effort to be charming and friendly in her company, and presumably he'd do the same when she returned. But he hadn't changed. He couldn't.

Flint sighed and flung a piece of glass. Five heads jerked, following its trajectory.

But things *were* changing in *his* life. He felt different.

'Here, girl.' Flint patted his leg.

The terrier looked round uncertainly at the other dogs.

'Come on.' Flint nodded.

Ears and tail twitched.

'You know you want to,' Flint coaxed. 'Come on.'

In one bound, the terrier leapt onto his lap and licked his face. Flint stroked and patted. The terrier curled, and lay down.

'Flint!' Dad's voice boomed off the walls of scrap. Dog ears twitched. *'Flint?'*

But it wasn't gruff. The tone was different: the rare, unnerving friendly voice. It wasn't a *summons*; Dad was coming to him. He was after something – more hard work probably. It was tempting to keep quiet and let him search . . .

Flint gave a shrill whistle.

Dad limped into view. 'Aha!'

'What's up?'

'Nothing. Ken's on the phone to a customer. I thought I'd come and see where you'd sneaked off to.'

Flint tickled the terrier's chin. Dad and Ken were up to something. Ken fenced stuff – he was behind Dad's going after the painting, no doubt about it.

Dad patted the Dobermann. 'That last Cup match . . .'

'The quarter-final.'

'Quarter-final, was it?' Dad's eyebrows twitched. 'Against . . . ?'

'Danvers.'

'Yeah – whatever. You won, didn't you? You're still in the competition?'

Flint nodded. 'Tough match.'

'So where does that put Beckton now?'

Why the sudden interest? 'We're through to the semis. Annesley. They've got a top coach, but a reputation for inconsistency.'

'Is that a home match, or away?'

'Home.' *What was his game?*

'Blast.' Dad frowned.

Flint was puzzled. 'You weren't thinking of coming along, then?'

'Unlikely.' Dad leant against a stripped-out van. 'And if you beat *them*? What about the final?'

'Tankerton, or Bridgehurst.'

'Home or away?'

'Sedgely Park – somewhere neutral. Both teams have to travel.'

'That's definite, is it?'

Flint nodded. 'And if we win the final,

124

there's the Cup-winner's Cup to look forward to then.'

'Too late,' said Dad.

'Too *late*?'

Dad shook his head. 'Anyway – there's no guarantees you'll get there. How d'you rate your chances against this next lot?'

'Annesley?' Flint shrugged. 'Hard to say, given their current form. Better than even, maybe? Why?' *What was Dad after?* 'What's going on?'

Dad took out his tobacco and began rolling a cigarette.

Flint fiddled with the broken dash. The familiar feeling, *unease*, was back. Dad wanted something from him . . . needed his cooperation . . . he was planning something. It had to be something *illegal*.

'The price has gone up for the painting.'

Oh no. Flint felt himself sinking.

Dad poked the cigarette between his lips. 'But there's a deadline. They need it by the end of the month. The customer's returning home. Abroad.'

The terrier lifted her head, glancing up at Flint through furrowed brows. Flint braced himself against the seat. 'Don't ask me to help.'

Dad lit the cigarette and blew a long plume of smoke. He stared.

Flint shivered. 'I'm just saying –' he snapped a piece of plastic from the dash – 'I don't want anything to do with it . . . break-ins and that. What you do is your business. But I don't want to be involved.'

'I think you'll find you're wrong.'

Flint stared back. 'Last time was the *last* time.'

'I don't think so.'

The fear was rising. 'What about our deal?' He knew it was hopeless. 'You said before that if I helped . . .'

Dad nodded. 'If you helped steal the painting, you got to carry on at Beckton Leigh.'

'I did. I did everything I could.'

'But I still don't have the painting.'

'That's not my fault.'

'No-one's saying it is. But *that* was the deal.'

'What if I've changed my mind?'

Dad stiffened. His eyes narrowed. 'You don't have that option.'

Flint nuzzled the terrier. 'We'll see,' he muttered.

'Come again?'

'Nothing.'

'So . . .' Dad flicked the fag end against a car door. The Dobermann sniffed and turned away. 'I've been racking my brains about how we're going to do it.'

'The painting?'

Dad nodded. There was a glint in his eye. 'They like their Cup matches, the Beckton families.'

'Some people enjoy football.'

Dad didn't blink. 'I've been sniffing around . . . Beckton's like a ghost village when you lads play away.'

'It's like a religion to them – the mums, dads, brothers and sisters, even aunts, uncles and grandparents.' Flint snapped a piece off the broken dash. Dad must once have felt just as passionate about the game. 'They all come along.'

Dad nodded. 'Suits us perfectly.'

'How d'you mean?'

'They go to the match. We pop round for a visit.'

'What? You mean . . .' Flint scowled. 'But what about the game? I'm supposed to be there!'

'Your teammates'll just have to survive without you.'

'But . . .' Furious words jammed in his throat. 'But . . . the *Cup final* . . . you *said*!'

'I said you could carry on playing for Beckton.' Dad pulled himself upright. 'Everyone misses the odd match – sick relatives and all that, or you could tell them you've got to help your dad out.'

'But this isn't any old match. You're asking me to give up the *final*!'

'That's right. There's still the league games.' Not a hint of concern. The face was stony, the eyes cold. 'If your team win, you'll have the Cup-winners to look forward to. There'll be a lot of empty houses in Beckton on Cup final day. We might even pay a few others a visit.'

'What?' Flint stared. 'You're raving!'

'Rob the rich.' Dad jingled the change in his pocket. 'Give to the poor!' He chuckled. 'Pretty nice houses, too. Could be treasure troves.'

Flint shrugged. 'I wouldn't know.'

'You can tell your coach after the semi-final.' Dad leered – it was almost a grin. 'Your gran's sick. I think she's had a stroke.' He turned. 'Right . . . I've a few bits and pieces to sort out with Ken. Don't be long.'

The piece of plastic snapped between Flint's fists with a loud crack. The terrier jumped to her feet and barked. Flint nuzzled. The dog licked his face.

What was he going to do? He'd already made up his mind not to help Dad any more. Now he had to carry that through.

The terrier skipped to the ground. Flint scrambled out of the wreck. He had to think of something. Fast.

think of something. Fast.

CHAPTER 13
ANNESLEY

Mr Russell banged his favourite locker.
'More cooperation, especially up front.' He
glanced at Rich. 'The midfield are your
support. Work *with* them. Defence . . .'

Flint pulled the laces tight. *Sabotage.*
That was the solution. Dad needed the
painting by the end of the month, but if
there were no away games before then – he
was *stuffed*.

'We've done well to come this far.' Mr
Russell smiled. 'But now we're here,
there's no reason we shouldn't take it all
the way.'

Flint poked mud clots from between
his studs. If Beckton lost this match, that
was it – no final, no away game. No silver-

ware for the club's cabinet, and no shot at the Cup-winners either. Could he wreck the team's chances? Was that in his power?

'If you play like you did in the second half against Danvers, Annesley won't have a chance. Let's pick up where we left off!' Mr Russell booted an imaginary ball. 'Get out there and give it to 'em!'

Flint had outrun the field.

'Take a shot!' yelled Mr Russell.

'Go on!' gasped Josh. 'What are you waiting for?'

Flint slowed. Just the keeper and one other player between him and the goal. The distance was comfortable. It wasn't a difficult angle – acres of netting to hit. Annesley's other defenders were still racing to block him. If he didn't act this second, the window would close . . .

'What are you *doing*?' bellowed Mr Russell.

Flint ran straight towards the goal. An Annesley boy moved to intercept. Good. Flint prepared himself. Stumble and lose possession. But, before he could drop, the defender crumpled in front of him. And before he could stop, he had skipped the defender's flailing legs and run on. *Blast*. Now he had to keep going.

Annesley's keeper was good. He had nerves of steel. Flint knew he could rely on him to give a good save.

'Take a shot, for God's sake!' Mr Russell's voice cut through supporters' cheers and shouts.

Flint glanced. On the other side of the box Rich was heavily marked. 'Rich!' He lofted the ball, up over incoming defenders, to land where Rich might reach.

The six-yard box was filling with black-and-white striped shirts. Undaunted, Rich dribbled, threading his way through the thicket of tackles. Flint raced towards the near post, signalling futilely for the ball. But just metres from the line, Rich whacked it. No chance for the keeper. Kissing the crossbar, the ball buried itself in the back of the net.

Rich raised his hands above his head.

'*Yes!*' roared the supporters.

Beckton's first goal of the match. It counted for a lot. But . . . Flint kicked the post. It *wasn't* supposed to have happened.

'At *last!*' bellowed Mr Russell. 'That's more like it!'

'Thanks!' Rich slapped Flint hard on the back. 'Seems like you finally got the message. Keep it up, *tramp*.' He turned and headed up the pitch.

Flint clenched his fists. Having to play like an idiot was bad enough. He didn't need Rich lording it over him.

'*Beckton*,' yelled the supporters. '*We want the Cup!*'

Josh jogged over. 'You had a clear open shot! What's got into you?'

Flint shrugged. 'We scored, didn't we?'

Josh's eyes flickered towards Rich. 'Is it him?'

Flint turned away. 'Don't be stupid.'

The eyes narrowed. 'What then?'

'I'm doing my best,' muttered Flint. Doing his best to play his worst. But it wasn't quite enough. Annesley's lead was meant to be unassailable by now. Instead, Rich's goal had made it a mere two goals to Beckton's one.

'*Flint!*' bellowed Mr Russell. 'Buck up your ideas – or you'll be *off*.'

Beckton returned to their own half, ready for renewed assault.

'One more, to catch them,' yelled Rich. 'We can do it.'

'Carefully now . . .' Mr Russell tapped his

forehead. 'No last-minute lunacy before the break.'

Annesley took their kick. Their strikers pushed up, ahead of the midfield; wingers brought the ball forward.

The moment the ball came back towards the centre, Flint struck – charging with a blind fury at the boy with ball. The blond striker went down.

'Ref!'

'*Penalty!*'

The whistle blew.

'What are you *doing*?' Josh grabbed Flint's collar. 'Idiot!'

The ref wagged a warning finger at Josh and waved him away. Then, reaching into his pocket, he showed Flint the yellow card. Flint bowed his head. His first offence with the team.

The ref pointed to the penalty spot. A cheer went up from the Annesley supporters.

'Sorry.' Flint held out his hand to the player on the ground.

The Annesley striker shrugged. 'Give away all the penalties you want, mate . . . suits us fine.'

Justin, in goal, tried to shake the tension from his legs. The blond striker rubbed his thigh. The whistle blew. He ran. Justin dived. The ball hit the back of the net.

'*What* is going on?' Mr Russell spread his hands in a gesture of exasperation. 'Perhaps it's something you all ate for breakfast?' He turned.

Flint met his gaze.

'If there's one thing that first half demonstrates, it's just how much of a linchpin you've become, Flint. Whatever you were doing before, you're not doing it now. And the result shows. What've you got to say for yourself?'

Flint could feel Rich's eyes, daggers across the changing room. 'I know I'm not playing my best . . . Everyone has off days . . .' He shrugged. 'I dunno . . .'

'I do have substitutes I could bring on.' Mr Russell gestured towards the B-team boys sitting in the corner.

'No . . .' Flint fumbled for the right thing to say. He couldn't be taken off. He had to stay in the game. He had to be convincing. 'I'll try harder, Coach . . . please.'

'You've been a liability so far. Why should I believe things'll be any different?'

'I've had stuff on my mind . . .' He looked

135

across at Rich. The eyes narrowed. 'My gran's not well . . . it's been a worry.'

Rich smiled.

'I'm sorry to hear that.' Mr Russell looked embarrassed. 'Nothing too serious, I hope . . .'

Flint bowed his head.

'Nevertheless . . .'

'Just another ten minutes,' said Flint. 'If my game doesn't pick up, then take me off.'

The silence was excruciating.

'OK. Ten minutes.' Mr Russell span on his heel. 'If any of you thinks that because Flint's been in the firing line, you can get away with poor play – think again. I can just as easily take one of you lot off.' Mr Russell clapped his hands. 'Right – let's have you on your feet!'

Studs clattered on the tiles. Boys crowded towards the door.

In the crush, Rich squeezed against Flint. He winked. 'Good boy,' he whispered. 'Now don't do anything *stupid*.'

Flint passed to Josh. Beckton had possession. Again. It had been back and forth, back and forth for more than twenty minutes. And no goals. He had managed to play convincingly enough to stay in the game, so far. But . . . something was niggling him.

Annesley players changed tack. Josh considered his options and crossed to André. Beckton pushed forward.

Flint advanced into the opposition half, keeping pace with his teammates. It had been murder trying to play badly. But trying to play just well enough to stay in the game was worse. His unease was deepening by the minute. *What was it?* It was *Rich* – the smile, the wink, the words. *That's* what was eating him.

André passed inside. Josh picked up the pace, darting past a stripy shirt and cutting in towards the centre.

Flint drove his legs faster. Rich believed he had got to him – that he was playing badly because he was afraid of Rich. Rich wasn't worried that the team were losing; he just wanted to be top-dog – king of the roost.

'Flint!' Josh slipped the ball sideways.

Flint surged, beat the Annesley midfielder, and cut left.

'Mind on the game,' intoned Mr Russell. 'Mind on the game.'

Rich was signalling up ahead. Flint

punted. A perfect pass. If you wanted to be top-dog, you had to *earn* it.

Making a short run to the edge of the box, Rich flicked the ball wide to Marcus.

'Go, Marcus – go!' Flint raced past Rich, heading for the six-yard line.

Rich accelerated, catching up. The cross came high and bending. Rich turned, jumped and brought the ball down. But his balance was thrown. He lost control. The ball bounced high.

Flint positioned himself. A defender dived, but he beat him to it. Full-blast . . . a power-kick, right from the hip.

'*Yeeeeees!*' The supporters went potty. '*Goooal!*'

'Yes, my son!' Marcus bear-hugged him, lifting him off his feet.

Josh made a fist and grinned. '*Now* you're showing your true colours!' All was forgiven.

Rich shot Flint an evil glance.

'*Come on, Beckton!*' yelled the supporters. '*We want more! We want more!*'

The teams jogged back for the kick. Flint shivered. It wasn't cold. It wasn't fear this time. He recognized the feeling – there was nothing quite like it. *Scoring!*

The whistle blew. Annesley charged,

four players in a line cutting through the Beckton ranks. André, Rich, Josh . . . Annesley kept on coming.

Flint retreated, eye on the ball, waiting for the moment.

Marcus went in hard. Annesley's winger barged past. He staggered, the ball drifted loose. Flint darted.

'*Yeees!*' roared Mr Russell from the touchline. 'Now make something of it.'

Flint ran. He felt good. He danced the ball round one player, slipped past a second. Ahead of him, André, Rich and Josh pushed forward. Stripy shirts fell back to block. Swerving through a gap, he flicked to Josh. He felt *electric*.

Josh passed wide. André launched into a clear run up the wing.

'*Beckton!*' yelled the supporters. '*Give us what we came for!*'

Now three of them were hurtling into the penalty area. Flint glanced sideways – four! Marcus was cutting in from the left. André lofted the ball. Josh chested it, dragging it away from the defenders.

The six-yard box loomed. Glancing back, Flint ran on.

Josh booted it. A low scudding ball, skipping as it came. Rich stretched a foot.

The ball arced up towards the crossbar. The keeper leapt – fisted the ball.

Flint hurled himself sideways, scissor-kicking as he fell.

'YEEEEEES!'

'Unbelievable!' Josh grabbed his face.

'What a turn-around!' André panted to a stop beside Rich.

'We can do it!' grunted Marcus, hefting Flint to his feet.

'Listen to yourselves!' sneered Rich. 'All worked up over a showy little trick.'

'Sour grapes!' hissed Josh. 'That was *no* showy trick.'

'*Craftsmanship*.' Marcus grinned. 'Pure *skill*!'

Rich glared.

'Come on.' Flint turned his back. 'We've still got a job to do.'

'*Come on, Annesley!*' yelled the supporters. 'Pull one back!'

And from the other side: '*Beckton, Beckton – one more goal!*'

They took up positions. Rich drifted towards Flint. 'What's the big idea, *tramp*? You haven't got the picture, have you?' He glared.

Flint froze. 'The picture?'

'Don't try and get smart with me.'

Rich jabbed a finger. 'Everyone thinks you're a thief! Most of them suspect you stole the stuff from the club. If they knew you were a filthy little liar too, d'you think you'd have a friend left? Have you forgotten what I said?'

Flint clenched his fists. 'What you said?'

Rich nodded. 'About telling people where you really live.'

Flint shook his head. Desperate means called for desperate measures. 'But . . . perhaps you've forgotten what *I* said?'

Rich frowned. 'What *you* said?'

Flint nodded. 'About a certain teddy?'

'You *what!*' Rich stumbled. His face darkened.

Flint held his stare. 'I think you know what I'm talking about.'

Rich's mouth opened, but no words came out.

The whistle blew. Suddenly stripy-shirts were advancing. Flint turned and ran to block them. He felt lighter on his feet. A change of tactics. This time the ball was coming straight up the middle – three players, passing short.

Flint tackled. The ball broke loose and rolled. Rich collected, forcefully. And took off.

'Go with him!' yelled Mr Russell. *'Take it all the way*, son.'

Beckton's front four tore after their captain. Stripy shirts chased.

Flint pumped his arms like pistons, driving his legs faster. Three . . . four . . . *five* players Rich had passed!

A sliding tackle, just outside the box. Rich dived. The ref shook his head. Desperate defenders collided in their rush to clear the ball.

Flint charged.

'Go, Flint!' yelled Josh, behind.

He hooked it loose, swivelled, and took off, zigzagging through the minefield. Stripy shirts to the left, stripy shirts to the right. And still he ran on – on towards the goal.

The supporters were screaming on both sides. No time to look for help. Ducking and barging, Flint made for a gap to his right.

The keeper crouched, sweating. Flint saw the fear in his face. *No mercy!* He grinned. And chipped.

It was over.

'A game of two halves – if ever there was one!' Mr Russell glowed with delight.

'Listen to them!' He nodded towards Beckton's supporters. 'They're over the moon. You lads gave one hell of a performance. Flint!' He stretched out his arms. 'What goals! What a boy!'

Flint grinned. 'The team were brilliant. It was the *team*.' Spotting Rich, he stretched out a hand. 'That last run was ... *dazzling*.'

Rich scowled and walked away.

CHAPTER 14
STUFFED

Flint sat up in his sleeping-bag. Dad's snores broke their even rhythm. He mumbled and shifted on the bed, then the rumble resumed. Flint sighed and pulled back the curtain.

Another restless night. Had he slept *at all*? He wiped condensation from the window and peered out. Another dismal, grey dawn.

He felt shattered. The knot in his stomach had been tightening all week. It practically throbbed to the touch. If ever there'd been a day he'd like to avoid, today was it. Maybe tomorrow the ache would be gone. But tomorrow seemed a long way off. He was stuck with the present.

He dropped back against the cushions. His original plan had been a good one. It was just a shame he'd changed his mind halfway through. The semi-final hadn't quite worked out as he'd intended.

It wasn't that he'd been *distracted* by Rich and his antics. But that had been the trigger. That was the moment he'd realized – sabotaging Beckton's chances wasn't something he could do. *Too late now*.

Flint unzipped his bag.

At that moment – the moment he'd decided to try and *win* – he had known there would be consequences. Today he had to face them.

The final was on. Beckton against Cup-holders, Bridgehurst. Picture-stealing, and possibly other crimes were on, too. Dad was depending on him to help out. Last week Dad had told him to inform Mr Russell he wouldn't be playing in today's match. But he'd disobeyed. When he'd decided to play to win, he'd known he must stand his ground.

Dragging on his jeans, Flint took another peep through the curtains: dismal and grey, but no sign of actual rain. Pity. All week he'd prayed that something would happen to delay the game – that it would rain till the end of the month, then Dad would be forced to abandon his plans and the showdown could be avoided. But it hadn't happened.

Rubbing warmth into his hands, he tiptoed to the cooker and lit the gas. It was best this way.

Coughing and grunting, Dad rubbed sleep from his eyes. 'What is this?' He swung his legs round under the table and sat upright. 'Some kind of joke?'

Flint shook his head.

Dad cupped his hands around the steaming mug. 'What d'you mean, you're not coming with me?'

'I'm not.' Flint sat on the couch opposite. 'I'm playing for Beckton.'

'But . . . we worked out the story you were going to tell the coach.' Dad reached for his tobacco. 'After the last match, you said—'

Flint bit his lip. 'I couldn't do it. They're relying on me.'

Dad's big fist came down *smack* on the table. '*I* was relying on you! I thought we were . . . a team.'

Flint watched the small puddle of tea spread slowly across the table. 'Sorry.'

Dad stared. '*Sorry?*' He laughed hard,

and coughed. 'Never be sorry, son. You've made your choice. Do what you've got to.' He pulled out some tobacco and began to roll. 'I'll have to manage without you.'

Flint shivered. 'How d'you mean?'

'What I said.' Poking the cigarette between his lips, Dad lit it. His face disappeared behind smoke. 'I'll do the job without you . . . I'll come home without you . . . and I'll carry on without you.' He dragged deeply and motioned towards the bedroom. 'Get your kit . . .'

'What?' Smoke billowed in Flint's face.

'You heard!' The eyes flashed. 'Get your kit . . . and get *out*!' Dad's finger thrust towards the door. 'Out! And don't come *back*.'

Just his luck. Flint stared down at the concrete bunker. Raindrops raked the puddle on its roof. The match could be cancelled. After all that! Water, dropping from high broken guttering, splattered against crumbling bricks. It sprayed and splashed him. Just his *sodden* luck.

He shivered and moved back inside the derelict house. Sky showed through holes in the ceiling. Only the room's too dark corners weren't already water-logged. His feet were soaked. He shivered some more. Everything was damp.

This might be his new home. This, or somewhere like it. There was no going back now. This was for real – out on his own.

Flint kicked at the rotten plaster. It crumbled and came away in big chunks. Dad had been in a furious state. Shouting and breaking things, hurrying him, dragging him to the door, literally throwing him out of the caravan.

He hadn't even had the chance to grab his watch. *What time had he left? How long had he been stuck out in the rain?* Could've been hours. Felt like days.

He rummaged in his rucksack. Under the circumstances, it wasn't surprising he hadn't packed a proper bag. He hadn't had a chance. He'd brought nothing. Not even a spare pair of socks. If he was going to survive on his own, he'd need more than football boots and shorts. More than a T-shirt and small towel. That was all he'd managed to grab before Dad flung him out.

The parking bay was empty. *Good*. No lights were on in the caravan.

Flint ran, splashing through puddles, across boggy grass to the steps. Inside, the air was still warm and smoky. Dad couldn't have been gone long. Broken glass crunched under foot. The place was even more of a tip than when he'd left. Bedclothes were scattered, the mirror was cracked and hanging at an angle. By the look of things, Dad had become a small whirlwind before leaving.

Just grab a few things.

Treading carefully in the half-light, Flint made his way to the bedroom. His foot brushed something. A scrunched-up ball of paper rustled and rolled towards the door. He crouched and unravelled it.

An unopened brown envelope. Their occasional mail had only ever been junk addressed to 'The Occupier', bills and mail for previous residents. Dad always threw it away unopened – that wasn't unusual. But this was actually addressed to Dad, *by name*. The back bore the details of the local doctor's surgery.

Flint frowned. Why hadn't Dad opened it? Tugging at the corner, he ripped it open and pulled out the letter.

Dear Mr Garside,
Following your recent tests at St Mary's Hospital, I would be grateful if

149

you could make an appointment to see me as soon as possible. Please be reminded of the advice given previously – you must avoid any strain on the lower back area and, in particular, must refrain from all lifting. In light of the test results, which I have now studied, I consider this advice imperative. Failure to heed it may result in permanent injury, even paralysis. I will discuss test results, diagnosis, prognosis and options for future treatment when I next see you in person.

Yours sincerely,

Dr Williams

Flint stared at the page. *Refrain from all lifting.* The letter didn't say what was wrong with Dad, but the tone of the letter – *imperative . . . permanent injury . . . paralysis* – that was *serious*.

An image flashed: a dark swirling storm, a monstrous sea, a man straining at the wheel of a battered boat. *The painting!* Dad was going to try to lift the painting off the dining-room wall. Alone! Even with two of them, it would've been heavy and difficult. But alone . . .

'Idiot!' Flint scrunched the letter into a tight ball and flung it at the wall. *I'll do the job without you . . . I'll come home without you . . . and I'll carry on without you.* If Dad tried to lift the painting, he'd do himself permanent injury – might even *paralyse* himself.

Flint stumbled over strewn clothes to his bedside table. No bets for guessing where Dad was right now. He rummaged for his watch. 10.37. If he got to a phone-box, there was still time to call the club – and what? Tell them he wasn't coming? Did he really have a choice now, knowing what he knew. He *had* to try and warn Dad. If he managed a convincing last-minute excuse to the coach, things might not be so bad – there was always a chance the match would be cancelled because of the weather. Grabbing what clothes came to hand, he stuffed them into his rucksack. *Why hadn't Dad opened the letter?*

Sixteen . . . seventeen . . . *eighteen* rings! Nobody was answering. The coach had left.

The match was on. He'd blown it. Double blown it.

Flint banged the handset back on its lip.

Stuffed. Three lousy phone-boxes, none of them working. And now that he'd found one that did, it was too late. The decision had been made for him. He was practically in Beckton village. What now? He knew what he *ought* to do.

The rain had started again. If only he could stay in the phone-box.

CHAPTER 15
BEECHCROFT REVISITED

Flint covered the rucksack with wet leaves and crept low between the trees. The house looked deathly still, shrouded in sleeting rain. He knew Dad was in there. The pickup was parked in the lane.

Stepping out of the beds, he hurried, *splash-splash*, across the lawn. He couldn't get more soaked, but at least the mud was being washed from his trainers. On the gravel outside the front door he halted.

Maybe he should ring the bell. If Dad was inside, he could've heard or seen him. Suddenly, for the first time, Flint felt scared. He climbed the steps. How would Dad react? What if he *wasn't* inside? What if someone else opened the door?

No. The coach was gone. Old Beckton was empty.

His fingers hovered over the small brass button. What if no-one answered?

Know your exit routes. Of course! If Dad was in there, the front door should be off the latch. Reaching for the handle, Flint twisted and gently pushed.

The door gave.

Taking a slow, deep breath, he entered and stood, letting the water run off onto the mat. The dining-room door was closed. All the doors off the hall were closed. Everything was in place. He eased the door shut.

Silence.

If Dad was here, he had heard him. He had heard the sound of the rain, and water dripping from the eaves. Now that the door was closed, the stillness was deafening.

Treading with the stealth his father had taught him, Flint bent his ear to the dining-room door and held his breath.

Nothing.

Perhaps Dad was on the other side, doing exactly the same thing?

Slowing his breath, Flint gripped the handle and turned. *Gently does it.* The door eased open. His eyes darted to the space on the wall. The painting – *gone!* Dad had managed it! He had cut away the canvas and . . . Crouching, Flint peered under the table.

He froze.

The painting sat propped against the wall. Dad lay sprawled by its side.

'Dad . . .'

Flint crawled. Dad's eyes were shut, his mouth open. The carpet was damp where he was lying. There was a wide, wetter patch around his hips. *'Dad . . .'* He touched the wetness. Warm. Not rain then. Sweat? Flint lifted his fingers to his nose. Uh-uh. *Wee.*

He touched Dad's arm. Cold. 'Dad?' The shoulder was limp to his prod. *'Dad!'* What were you supposed to do? Check there was a heartbeat? He dug his hand inside the jacket. *Where was the pulse?*

Where?

Thank God. Less than half the speed of his own, but still there. *Not dead then.* His own pulse was going way too fast. Panic. *Calm down.* At moments like this, it was important to think clearly. Check for breath. Breath was important. He put his ear up close to the open mouth. *Breathing.* Slightly, and . . . very slowly.

Flint took a long, deep breath.

He looked around. *What had happened?* There were no marks on the wall and no apparent damage to the painting – nothing to suggest it'd been dropped. Dad must've lowered it all the way to the floor. Then collapsed after.

Again Flint checked Dad's breathing. Was this the paralysis the doctor's letter had warned of? *Avoid any strain on the lower back . . . refrain from all lifting.*

'Dad . . .' Flint put a hand against the rough cool cheek and gently . . . slapped. The mouth gaped. Nothing. He tried again, harder this time. 'Dad . . . wake up!' No response. This was insane. He hadn't a clue – Dad could be *dying*. He had to get help. He had to get Dad to hospital.

He scrambled for the door.

A sound, more grunt than speech, made him turn. 'Flint?' A familiar cough.

He rushed back. 'Dad?'

'Jeeeez . . .' The frail, hoarse voice didn't sound like Dad at all. He blinked and squinted. 'What's happened?'

Flint knelt. 'You've had some kind of accident. Lifting the painting off the wall.' He leant close. 'Do you remember?'

'I did it,' Dad gasped. 'I got it down.' The

head lifted. 'After that . . . I . . . I forget.' He closed his eyes, shifted an arm and dropped his head forward. The face tightened with strain. Nothing else moved. He winced, gasped and fell back.

'You need a hospital.' Flint's eyes flitted. Dad's followed to the damp patch on the carpet. '*Christ* . . . I've pissed myself.' The frown deepened. 'How come you're here?'

'I went back to the caravan – for dry clothes.' Flint looked up. 'I found your letter.'

'Letter?'

'From the doctor.'

Dad's head lifted again. 'Letter from the doctor?' He winced, grunted and fell back.

'Why didn't you *open* it?' Flint clenched his fists. The anger in his own voice scared him. 'I read it. That's how come I came looking for you.'

Dad frowned.

'It said *not to lift*.' His words were bullets. 'Under *any* circumstances. The doctor had the test results. You might be paralysed.'

Dad winced. 'I don't think so.'

'This needn't have happened –' Flint's voice cracked – 'if you'd *read* it.'

Dad snorted. 'Surprised you haven't

157

worked that one out, living with me fifteen months – perhaps you're *not* so smart.'

'What?' Flint scowled.

'I never learnt.'

'Learnt?'

'To *read*, genius.' Dad grimaced. '*Aaaaagh!* That hurts.'

Dad couldn't read. Flint stared. *Dad was in agony*. 'You need to get to a hospital. You shouldn't be trying to move. I'm going to call an ambulance.'

'Don't be stupid *all* your life!' Dad coughed. 'An ambulance? Pick me up here?' He gestured feebly with his arm. 'How am I going to explain?'

Flint shrugged. 'I don't know. Maybe you won't have to.' He headed for the hall. 'But right now, I don't see that there's much choice.'

'Wait!' Dad gasped.

Flint turned.

'Please . . . there's no point you being dragged into all this.' Dad beckoned. 'Bring the phone here. If it'll reach.'

The cable, stretched to its limit, wasn't quite long enough. Flint put the phone by Dad's feet. 'Just about.'

'Pass me the receiver. You dial.'

Flint punched the button – 9 . . . 9 . . . 9.

Dad nodded. 'It's ringing.'

Flint felt his mind stray. Everything suddenly seemed so normal – him and Dad together in someone else's house.

'Hello . . . ambulance, yeah – I need an ambulance . . . it's an emergency . . . OK . . .' Dad cupped his hand over the mouthpiece. 'They're putting me through!' He winced. 'Good job I'm not bleeding to death!'

Flint smiled. Dad's first joke. Was this what it took?

'Yeah . . . oh, hello, yeah – I've had a fall, I can't move my legs. No, I'm not sure I can even feel them. I've got pain in my back . . . excruciating . . . Yeah, that's right, I think I need an ambulance . . .' Dad covered the mouthpiece again. 'So far, so good.'

Flint nodded.

'The address?' Dad grunted with pain. 'Beechcroft Mansions, Old Beckton . . . big gates, the corner of Crabtree Lane and the green. No, the gates are open. Don't move?' A wince. 'Don't worry . . . not likely to. No, I'm on my own. Thanks. OK . . . Bye . . .' He held out the receiver.

Flint clicked the line.

'They're coming.' Dad grunted and lay back. 'You best get out of here.'

'I'll wait.'

'You won't!'

Flint held Dad's stare.

'Don't be stupid. What are you going to do – help me onto the stretcher?'

Flint shook his head. 'I can hide when they get here. You need someone with you till they come, in case anything happens.'

'I'll be fine. I'm sure they're perfectly capable –' Dad struggled for a smile – 'so long as you make sure they can get in. The gate panel's behind the curtain, to the left of the door. Top button.'

'I'll see to it.' Flint carried the phone back to the hall. Behind the curtain he pressed the top button and watched from the window. At the bottom of the drive the gates swung open. As distant sirens wailed, he returned to the dining room.

Dad had shifted onto his back. 'They're going to do me for this.' His voice rasped and he coughed. 'There's no sense you getting into trouble.' The words were barely more than a mumble. 'Make sure you slip away unseen . . . take my bag . . . go back to the caravan.' The head lolled.

'Dad . . .' Flint scurried. He bent to Dad's chest. Still breathing – very slowly. Unconscious.

The sirens were growing closer.

160

Checking the room one last time, Flint grabbed Dad's bag and ran to the front door.

Blue lights flashing, an ambulance turned through the gates. Flint pulled the door ajar, turned and headed for the stairs.

CHAPTER 16
RICH

Flint slumped. He felt like he did after losing a tough game. Physically *and* mentally drained – all that running around in the rain, all that nervous energy, all that trying and trying . . .

Then *defeat*.

He'd racked his brains, trying to think of a way to get the picture back on the wall. He was a fool. He should have left straight after the ambulance. It was risky to have stayed this long. *Very*.

Daylight, what little there'd been of it, was fading fast. That's how late it was. He checked his watch. The final must have gone ahead, in spite of the weather. At the back of his mind he'd been hoping against hope for a water-logged pitch. But the Langston-Prannetts would've been home by now. He'd been so busy worrying about Dad, he'd not had time to think what *he* had sacrificed. Who he'd let down.

If, instead of returning to the caravan, he'd gone straight to the game, what would've happened? He would have played in the final, but Dad might have died. When the Langston-Prannetts came home, they'd have found him, lying by the painting.

At least Dad had got to hospital.

The Langston-Prannetts would contact the police – they were bound to, when they saw the painting. The call to the ambulance would be discovered. And that would lead them straight to Dad. With his record – plenty of related previous, *and* the suspended sentence – he'd be looking at a heavy stretch.

'Idiot!' *Why hadn't Dad told him he couldn't read or write? What a twisted man.* 'What an *idiot*!'

The word filled the empty hall.

If Dad had to go to prison, *he* would be 'taken into care'. Children's homes, and, if he was lucky, foster parents. Or – he could do what he'd been planning to do when Dad kicked him out.

Which was what exactly?

He should go. It was only tiredness that kept him from getting up and walking out the door. That, and the fact that, once again, it was chucking it down outside. It seemed a shame – his clothes were just about dry. He pulled himself up by the banister.

One last thing.

Smiling, he climbed the stairs. One last thing. *The teddy*. He owed himself a quick look. He wanted to see it in the light. Then he'd leave.

He padded along the landing, opened the door, and switched on the light.

Pink? Flint burst out laughing. *'Pink!'* Dropping onto the bed, he picked up the teddy. Rich slept with a *pink* teddy. This was too much!

He looked around at Rich's room. Not as spick and span as the rest of the house, but very neat and tidy for a boy. It was bigger than it'd seemed in the dark. The walls were decorated with posters of Man United and England and the teams' star players. There was a TV and playstation. Luxury.

He lay back on the soft bed and, chuckling to himself, clasped the teddy to his chest. He closed his eyes.

*　*　*

What was that? Flint woke with a start. Light dazzled his eyes. He glanced at his watch. *Oh no!*

Voices. A door slamming. *Oh God . . .* the Langston-Prannetts were home! Flint slipped off the bed and crept to the door.

'OK, kids!' A sharp woman's voice. 'Ready for bed. Clean your teeth and wash – *properly.*'

Voices and footsteps on the stairs. Rich and his sister.

Panic. Flint squeezed the door shut and scanned the room. *Where could he hide? The wardrobe?* Under the bed would be quieter. He turned off the light, and fumbled through the dark, arms outstretched.

Where was it? Shoving Dad's bag under the valance, Flint shuffled in behind.

The door opened. Light clicked on. A kit-bag thudded on the floor.

At last!

The thin sliver of light vanished under the door, leaving total darkness.

Flint shifted a leg. Snores rumbled above, soft and untroubled. It'd been the most excruciating wait of his life – listening to Rich getting ready for bed, Rich tossing and turning on the mattress above. Not moving in case he was heard; not allowing himself to get comfortable in case he fell asleep.

Then he'd had to endure Mr and Mrs Langston-Prannett nattering and moving about downstairs for what had seemed like *hours*. Finally, locking up, they had gone to bed, oblivious to the dining-room's secret. Flint sighed. He had aged.

Stupid – to have got into this mess. He felt like laughing. Nerves.

Flexing life into dead fingers and feet, he slid hands in front of his face and pressed the light button on his watch. 22.47. Give it half an hour – *then leave.*

He stretched – *half*-stretched: there wasn't enough space, the cavity under the bed was cluttered with stuff. Carefully shifting position, he set to, making room in the dark.

He felt with his fingers. What was *that* – a stiff sock? *Phew!* He could *smell* it too. He pushed it away, hooking it down with his foot.

He probed again . . . something cold, hard and smooth . . . curved . . . and flat. A plate! It had something on it that felt like

166

... *eurgh* ... the furry remains of food! How long had *that* been there? Dragging the plate towards his knees, he nudged it aside.

Once more he sent reluctant fingers exploring. A smelly trainer ... another – its partner? A baseball cap ... a paperback with something *sticky* on it – *disgusting!* He moved each item down towards the bottom end, slowly but surely excavating Rich's secret rubbish tip.

What was *this*? Something cold, hard and smooth again ... curved too ... but not as thick as the plate, nowhere near. Fingers explored further. A deep bowl ... it had handles, a stem and a base. This was a shape he recognized.

A trophy.

What was that doing here? Why hide a trophy?

Flint dragged the trophy to one side and probed deeper. His heart galloped. Something cold and hard again. He groped. Curved ... handles ... a stem and base ... *Another* trophy!

His fingers were hurrying now; they crawled through the darkness once again. A tennis ball ... a mug ... another trainer ... then ... *there it was!* A flat heart-shaped piece of wood . . . cold metal plaques. Two trophies and now *this*. The Team Captain's Shield! *It had to be!*

Beckton's trophies under Rich's bed. This changed things. *But – how?* There was no way to be sure it was them. Not without putting the light on.

What now?

Flint stretched – properly this time – lying back and listening for the snores.

Rich had tried to point the finger at him for stealing the silverware. And the wallet – it was probably here too, somewhere under all the mess. It'd been part of Rich's little campaign, trying to turn the team against him. Rich was shiftier than he'd credited. It'd been clear he had taken an instant dislike to him and clear he resented having new competition on the side, but to go to *these* lengths – that was really *desperate*.

Everyone has hidden depths, hidden secrets.

Flint poked his head out from under the valance, relishing the fresher air. By stealing the trophies, Rich had risked losing everything he had with the club. *Perhaps he believed that was happening anyway?*

It made sense. They *had* to be the missing trophies.

Rich's snores broke rhythm. He mumbled and shifted, the snores resumed.

Easing the rest of his body out from under the bed, Flint crouched. He focused on Rich's breathing. *As long as that stayed regular* . . . Feeling with outstretched arms, he found the duvet and slid his hand up over the shape of Rich's chest, towards the snores.

An arm . . . up past the teddy . . . Rich's chin.

Very gently, Flint positioned his hand where he could feel the breath. With his other, he groped for the bedside light. Three . . . two . . . one . . .

Light.

Clasping his hand tight over Rich's mouth, Flint jumped and straddled.

Rich writhed and jerked, his eyes stretched wide in shock and panic, blinking against the light.

Flint bore down with all his weight and brought his face up close. '*Listen!*' he hissed.

Rich's legs kicked and twisted under the duvet.

'*Struggle any more –*' Flint pressed his

arm down hard against Rich's throat – 'and I'll wake your parents.' He spoke in a half-whisper. 'Do you want that? Do they know what's under the bed?'

Rich's body went rigid. His eyes bulged.

Flint shook his head. '*No?*' He tutted and wagged a finger. 'Keeping secrets from Mummy and Daddy. Very *naughty*.'

Rich's arm muscles flexed furiously. His legs thrashed.

Flint thrust down hard, still gagging the mouth, bracing against the throat. 'I'm not *kidding* . . .'

Rich gasped. His face turned crimson.

'*Relax!*' grunted Flint. '*Now*. Or the parents wake!'

Fierceness flickered in the eyes. Slowly, the body went limp.

'That's better.' Flint slackened his grip just a touch. '*Keep it that way*.' He put a finger to his lips. 'I'm going to take my hand from your mouth. *Not a sound*.'

Rich stared up at him in silent fury.

'Good.' Flint eased off his weight. 'OK, now listen – in a minute, you're coming downstairs with me. I need your help with something.'

A twisted smile spread across Rich's face. 'I was *right* about you.'

Flint felt his fists clench and his whole body tighten. Rich was helpless beneath him – smashing his mocking, grinning face would be . . . *such* a release. He took a slow deep breath, and stared into the hate.

Rich's sneer faltered.

Don't do it.

Rich blanched.

Flint felt his muscles unclench. He shook his head. 'You were wrong.' He put a warning finger to Rich's lips and gave his cheek a gentle slap. 'Already you've forgotten our little deal.' Shifting his weight, he swung a leg to the floor. 'It shouldn't take long.' He climbed off. 'Silent cooperation. You know the score.'

Rich sat up, awkwardly trying to conceal the teddy; a little pathetic in his blue pyjamas.

'OK . . .' Flint eased the door and put his ear to the crack. Gentle snores floated down the landing. He beckoned to Rich. 'Do you have a torch?'

Rich nodded.

'We'll need it.'

Rich crossed the room, and came back with a bicycle light.

'Good.' Shouldering Dad's rucksack, Flint nodded towards the stairs. 'Let's go.'

Silently, stealthily, they descended. At the bottom of the stairs Flint pointed the light. 'Dining room,' he whispered.

Rich unlocked the door. The two boys entered. Flint led the way to the painting. Rich stared.

'I could be a thief —' Flint sighed — 'but I'm *not*. We're putting the painting back.' He pointed. 'Grab your corner.'

The two boys positioned themselves.

'One . . . two . . . three . . . heave!'

They strained . . . and lifted. It was *heavy*! They held it, puffing to stifle their grunts.

Flint's fingers fumbled blindly at the back. He searched for the wire. 'Got it!'

Done.

The two boys slumped.

'You broke in here and did this —' in the gloom, Rich's face had a gaunt haunted look — 'just to show me you're *not* a thief?'

Flint shrugged.

Rich shook his head. 'Nah . . .'

Flint shone the light at the picture. The man adrift in a storm had a crazed glint in his eye. Flint lowered the beam to the plaque at the bottom. He looked at Rich.

Rich sneered. 'What?'

'Read it.'

'*A Certain Kind of Courage* . . . ?'

Flint shone the beam in Rich's face. 'People are going to notice a change in you.'

Rich frowned.

Flint turned towards the door. 'They'll see you trust and respect me.' His voice sounded tired. Shining the light into the hall, he spotted the front door. 'They'll see you're not afraid,' he whispered. He clicked off the torch.

Total darkness.

'Sweet dreams.'

CHAPTER 17
CUP FINAL

Sunlight dappled the table. Flint dashed soft bristles, back and forth, over the leather.

Funny . . . *that night* – he'd never thought to ask Rich about the final. Too preoccupied, too busy *worrying* . . .

Placing the boot next to its companion, Flint lay back against the cushions and admired the results of his hard work. They positively *gleamed*. He was ready.

Ready for the rescheduled final.

His eyes strayed around the caravan. Tidy.

A knock at the door. Flint jerked upright, and leant his face against the window. 'Saff!' He tapped. 'Come in! It's open.'

The door clunked. The familiar warm

smile. 'Hiya!' Saff held out her arms. 'Did you *miss* me?'

'Badly!' Flint stood and hugged. 'Like you couldn't imagine.'

Saff laughed.

'When did you get back?'

'Just now.' She glanced at her watch. 'I set off at first light. I've been at the tiller for . . . crikey . . . *five* hours. My *God!*' Her eyes widened, her mouth dropped. 'What happened to the caravan? It looks clean and neat!'

Flint smiled, nodded. 'I'll make some tea.' He gestured. 'Put your feet up.'

'Somebody's turned over a new leaf.' Dragging a finger across the table, Saff examined it for dirt. 'Your hard work, no doubt. And what about your dad?'

Flint shrugged.

'Has he been . . . keeping his promises?' Saff raised an eyebrow. 'Has he . . . kept out of *trouble*?'

Flint warmed the pot. 'Better ask him yourself.'

'Where is he?'

Deep breath. 'Hospital.'

'What!' Saff's hands leapt to her face.

Flint nodded. 'His back . . . his spine – the *injury*. He collapsed over in Old Beckton.'

'Oh, my *God*! Have you seen him? Is he all right?'

He nodded again. 'Not bad considering . . . as well as can be expected, the doctors say.'

'Considering *what*?'

'The nerves to his legs were trapped, pinched by bone or something. They were practically severed . . . but now they've operated there's a good chance of recovery.'

Saff bit a nail. 'How did it happen?'

'I'm not sure.' Flint shrugged. 'Dad'll tell you all about it.'

Saff's eyes probed. 'That's what you'd rather?'

He nodded. 'You don't mind?'

'No . . . no – I understand.' She sighed. The frown deepened. 'I . . . I should go and see him . . . I suppose.'

'Visiting time's not for an hour. He's been there a week . . . his condition's stable, but he won't be going anywhere.' Flint raised the teapot. 'Have some tea first.'

'Yes – sensible idea.' Saff pulled up her legs, and attempted to settle in the cushions. 'I think a situation like this requires two sugars – *please*.'

Flint poured.

'So . . . what's it been like, without him

176

around? How've you been coping?'

'Good . . . to be honest.' Flint glanced. 'I lied at the hospital – said I was Dad's nephew. I was worried social services might get hold of me.' He tapped his head. 'Touch wood, no-one's come snooping. It's been a little quiet, but now that you're back . . .'

Saff smiled. 'What about money – how've you been managing?'

'I got myself a job. Dad's mate Ken found me some work, helping out at the scrap-yard. Part-time stuff, but enough for rent and food.'

'Enterprising.'

'Had to be. Dad's not going to be bringing money in.' Flint stirred the tea. 'He thinks he is, but then – *he* thinks he's going to be back living in the caravan in a few more days.'

'And that's not realistic?'

Flint shook his head. 'Nerves can regrow, but very slowly – a millimetre a day. His have got a long way to go. Maybe you can talk some sense into him. I've tried.' He clinked the teaspoon on the side of the mug. 'He's going to be in a wheel-chair, for starters. Then crutches – if he's *lucky*. A caravan's out of the question.'

'He needs help . . . from social services.'
Saff unzipped her jacket. 'I can go to an
advice centre. He might qualify for a flat –
the council or some other agency. There
must be benefits he can claim.'

Flint nodded. His turn to do the eye
probe. *Saff knew Dad – did she know about
the reading and writing?*

'You think I'm mad to try, don't you?'

'No.'

Saff fiddled with her zip.

'Here.' Flint placed mugs on the table.
'Two sugars.'

'Thanks.' Saff cupped the warmth.
'Listen – I realize what a hard time you've
been having this last year. I just want you
to know – depending how things pan out
with your dad and everything, you can
come and stay with me if ever . . . *whenever*
you need.'

'Thanks . . .'

'I mean it.' Her eyes said she did. 'So . . .
Mr Coping Capable Enterprising! How did
you get the job?'

'It's *who you know!*' Flint laughed. 'With
Dad being out of action, I think Ken felt
responsible.'

Saff's eyes probed again.

Let her find out from Dad. 'There's

more work next week, if I want it.'

Saff shook her head. 'We have to do something about getting you in school.'

Flint grinned. 'The scrapyard dogs have been the *best* company.' He dribbled an imaginary ball round imaginary dogs, barking and yapping.

'Hey!' Saff laughed. 'You've been honing your football skills!'

'Always practising!' Flint nodded to the window sill – *the boots*. 'Today's Cup final day!'

'The *Cup final*!' Saff's face lit up. 'I thought it was *last* weekend?'

Flint nodded. '*Sleeted* off in the last twenty minutes! Luckily for me.' He shivered. 'Dad was admitted to hospital. I missed the coach.'

Saff raised her eyes heavenward and smiled. 'Someone looking out for you?'

'Maybe.'

'But that's brilliant.' She sipped her tea. 'At least there's some good news. How you getting on with your good friend . . . Richard?'

'Rich?' Flint felt a smile pulling at his lips. A wry grin.

'Oh my God!' Saff glanced at her watch. 'The Cup final's this afternoon?

179

What time's kick-off?'

'Two. Over at Sedgely Park.'

Saff sipped, slurped . . . *gulped* her tea.
'I should get a move on, if I'm going to visit
your dad.'

Flint nodded.

'But I *promise* –' she jumped to her feet
– 'I'll do my *utmost* to get there.'

Grabbing his jacket, Flint rummaged
in the pockets. 'Here . . . these might
help.' He tossed the pickup keys across the
table.

Saff's eyes narrowed. 'Mr Coping
Capable Enterprising . . . ?'

'Ken drove it back.' Flint winked, pure
mischief. 'Believe me!'

'OK.' Mr Russell nodded to the driver.

Josh nudged Flint. 'Here we go!'
Underneath them, the engine rumbled
into life.

Mr Russell cleared his throat. 'On this –
a most *auspicious* occasion for Beckton
Leigh –' he touched hand to heart; boys
nudged and prodded one another – 'it
gladdens me to have *good* news to
announce . . . for a change.'

Boys cheered and whistled.

Mr Russell grinned triumphantly. 'The

club's missing silver has been returned!'

Louder cheers and whistles.

'On this matter –' Mr Russell held up his hands for quiet – 'your captain would like to say a few words.'

Heads swivelled, bodies twisted. At the back of the bus Rich's head was bowed.

'Tell the team what you told me, Richard.'

Slowly, the head lifted. Pale. He cleared his throat. 'I was first to arrive this morning. When I got here, someone was climbing into a car. It drove off – a man, I think. I found the trophies against the wall.'

Cheers. Fists punched the air.

Rich nodded. His eyes flickered to Flint. 'I feel . . .' He cleared his throat again. 'I feel . . . I owe Flint an apology . . .'

The coach engine revved, filling the silence.

'*Ooooh!*' gasped the supporters.

Rich fell. The whistle blew. The ref signalled a free kick.

'Oh, come on!' yelled Flint. The stocky midfielder had felled Rich twice before.

'Send him *off*!' yelled Beckton's supporters. 'Come on, *ref*!'

'*Bridgehurst!*'

'*Beckton Leigh!*'

The player held his hand out to Rich. Rich scowled, muttered and waved him away.

'*Bridgehurst!*'

'*Beckton Leigh!*'

The player muttered something back and walked away. Suddenly, Rich had jumped to his feet, fists clenched. Josh, red-headed Chris and a couple of Bridgehurst's players dashed in. Shaking a finger, the ref forced them apart.

'*Bridgehurst!*'

'*Beckton Leigh!*'

Flint hurried over. It was the biggest, noisiest crowd he had ever played for – Beckton's supporters vying cheer-by-cheer with the massed opposition. The two groups had competed non-stop since before kick-off, filling the stadium with the two teams' names. Beckton's supporters had held their own.

Which was more than could be said for the team. 3–0 down, with only a few minutes to the half-time whistle. Tempers were fraying, spirits sinking. Beckton had been giving it their all . . . and getting nowhere.

'Who's taking it?' said Flint.

'Too far out for me,' said Rich. 'But if you think you can do it . . .'

Flint stared.

'It's practically half the pitch!' said Marcus.

'We're running out of time.' Rich nodded towards the big clock. 'If we don't score in two minutes . . .'

'There'll be no point coming out for the second half.' Josh spat. 'Take a shot!'

Flint nodded.

Rich placed the ball on the mud. '*Make it special.*'

Flint measured his paces, blew on his hands, focused . . . Rich had just asked him to make it special! That called for something extra.

A short blast on the whistle.

He ran. Leather smacked against leather – boot against ball . . .

It soared . . . bending round the last man on the wall . . . over the keeper's outstretched hands and . . . *under the crossbar*.

'Has to be goal of the season,' said Mr Russell.

Flint lowered his head, embarrassed.

'So far!' chuckled Rich.

'Certainly couldn't have come at a more crucial time.' Mr Russell paced the tiles. 'I warned you this lot'd be tough. A team doesn't make three finals in a row without having something. *What's been going wrong?*'

Everyone spoke at once – a dozen different viewpoints of the game.

'Whoa!' Mr Russell raised his hand. 'One at a time, please. Let's hear what we have to say.'

'They've got a skin-tight defence,' said Marcus.

Josh nodded. 'And fully-formed giants for forwards.'

'That's not the problem,' said Rich. 'We're a match for them under *fair* conditions. But we're not getting a chance. Look how many free kicks've been given! The referee's the problem.'

Heads nodded.

'Bridgehurst are playing dirty. And he's letting them get away with it. If he'd done his job properly – booking players and sending them off – by now they'd be down to half a team.'

'Rich is right,' said Flint. 'If we'd had the penalties we deserved, the scores would be equal. He should've shown *twenty* yellow cards, not two.'

'OK,' said Mr Russell. 'We're stuck with the ref – so what do we do?'

'Play a different game,' said Marcus.

Mr Russell nodded.

'Don't give them the opportunities,' said Rich.

'That's right!' Mr Russell tapped an imaginary ball. 'Pass early whenever possible. Don't be tempted to play *their* game. Play hard, but keep it clean. Right!' He clapped his hands. 'On your feet . . .'

Studs clattered.

Mr Russell stood by the changing-room door. 'We've scored a *dazzling* goal. It's just the start –' he made a fist – 'the start of a *rout*. We're going to turn things around. Teamwork has been the best I can remember – truly *excellent*. All of you have risen to the occasion. You've been the better team, without doubt. Now, let's get out there . . . and *take what we deserve!*'

The team crowded, cheering, towards the exit.

Rich moved towards Flint. 'What's that I smell?'

Flint stared.

Rich stared back. He grinned. 'Mmm . . .

smells like *team spirit*. Let's score some goals!'

Flint grinned. 'You bet!'

An icy rain had come and gone during the first half, turning the pitch into a quagmire, and Bridgehurst's all-white strip muddy brown. Now, a gentle breeze was blowing. Pale blue sky glimmered through the cloud.

'Beckton!'

'Bridgehurst!'

Supporters from both sides urged on their teams, with louder and louder chants.

'BECKTON!'

'BRIDGEHURST!'

Playing the passing game cautiously, but well, Beckton had finally notched a second goal. Marcus's first goal of the season, off a cross by Josh. It was time to raise the tempo.

Rich and Flint raced neck-and-neck up the middle, Josh and Marcus close behind, Nicholas and André on the wings. Rich passed to Flint. Bridgehurst were on the back foot: they had switched to defence; the field ahead was thick with muddy white. Flint paused – allowing Josh to overtake – then passed and moved up. Ahead, Marcus entered the box.

Josh cut right, leading defenders away. 'Flint!'

The ball came back. Flint accelerated, swerved to avoid a tackle and tapped across to Marcus. *'One-two!'*

Nicholas and André were swooping from the sides. Rich had crossed the six-yard line. Bridgehurst were piling back *en masse*. Flint sprinted.

'Flint!'

The ball scudded the mud. Flint turned and charged. Bridgehurst hurled themselves, helter-skelter, in his path.

No way but *through*. Head down, Flint ducked and barged, swerved, ducked and barged again. *Where were the red-and-golds?* There! 'Rich!' He chipped.

Rich leapt. And headed.

'Gooooal!'

The keeper hit the mud.

'Beckton! Beckton! We're going to win the Cup!'

Beaming, Rich held out his palm. Flint slapped it. 'We've equalized!'

Josh and Marcus grinned.

Laughing, punching the air, cartwheeling, the four boys raced back to their half.

'*Come on, Bridgehurst!*' yelled the opposition supporters.

'*Beckton! Beckton!*' yelled the Beckton crowd. '*One more goal! Beckton! Beckton! We want THE CUP!*'

Underneath the two groups' raucous shouts, Flint picked out another chant. '*Here we go . . . here we go, here we go . . .*' He looked over towards the touchline. Those voices . . . he recognized . . .

Saff . . . and *Dad*! Dad had had a haircut and was wearing new clothes.

'Go on, my *son* . . .' From a wheelchair, Dad waved and punched the air.

Flint stared . . . shook himself . . . smiled.

The whistle blew. Action. Bridgehurst took their kick and pushed forward.

'Watch the wings!' yelled Rich.

A change of tactics: instead of pushing up the middle, as they had done before, Bridgehurst's forwards spread the ball wide. Their winger passed Nicholas on the left. Flint, Josh and Marcus fell back.

'I'm taking him,' yelled Flint. He felt light. He felt fast. He raced to block the player's path.

The winger cut in. Flint switched trajectory, diving feet-first for the ball.

'Mine!' Snatching possession, Marcus bolted.

Bridgehurst slammed on the brakes.

'Let's do it!' yelled Rich from the front.

'Here we go . . . here we go . . . here we go . . .' Beckton's supporters leapt up, waving and chanting, Saff and Dad at the front of them. Flint felt his heart skip a beat. Saff was beaming from ear to ear, willing the team to victory, willing him to do something that little bit special. *'Here we go . . . here we go . . . here we GO-OH!'*

Passing the ball between them, Nicholas, Marcus and Josh advanced into opposition territory. Flint gave chase.

With the roar of Beckton's supporters in their ears, Bridgehurst scrambled back to their goal-line, squawking and flapping like chickens.

Nicholas was down. Still in possession, Marcus and Josh pushed on through Bridgehurst's disarray.

'Josh!' Flint shot past them on the left, thundering into the box. The ball came over – beautifully judged – no need to slow or change direction. He ploughed on, round one . . . two . . . *three* . . . glanced across . . . hooked it . . . *'Rich!'*

189

Rich chested the ball, swivelled on the six-yard line, and *whacked* it.

Dunk!

Off the crossbar, the ball ricocheted *up* . . .

Flint staggered in front of the goal.

. . . *up and back* . . .

He dropped his hips.

The ball fell.

He *leapt* . . .

. . . flipping back . . .

. . . reaching foot to sky . . .

. . . belting the ball . . .

. . . somersaulting . . .

'*Yeeeees!*' It was there.

THE END

If you enjoyed this book, why not try
another from the same author – *Brooksie*.

Imagine being the son of one of England's
top strikers . . .
Now imagine your famous father losing form
and becoming the laughing-stock of the
whole country . . .
That's what happens to Lee Brooks.

*Now turn over for the first action-packed
chapter . . .*

BROOKSIE

NEIL ARKSEY

CHAPTER 1

MATCH POSTPONED

Lee Brooks kicked the bench. What a pathetic first half! He'd been worse than useless. Again.

'Right! Gather round and listen.' Mr MacKay glared and puffed out his big chest. 'In case you'd all forgotten – this is the final.'

Lee tried to focus on Mr MacKay's words, tried to concentrate.

'We've had our ups,' said Mr MacKay, 'and this season, Lord help us, we've had our downs. But it's the end of the school year and we're here!' He whacked his palm against a locker. 'That's of no consequence if we fail to score in the next thirty-five

195

minutes. To take home that cup we need *goals.*'

Sheepish nods all round.

'Over in the other changing room,' said Mr MacKay, 'their coach is probably saying the exact same thing, so bear in mind – we need *more goals than them.*'

More nods and murmurs.

'Brooks . . .'

Lee bit his lip. Everyone looked down at the floor; they knew what was coming.

'. . . same thing I've been nagging you about all term.' Mr MacKay's tone softened slightly. 'I know you've had a lot on your mind . . .'

Slight understatement! Lee nodded. 'Yes, sir.'

'. . . especially today, with your father so much in the spotlight . . .'

Dad's first game in months. Last game of the season. Last chance.

'. . . but that doesn't alter the fact that out there,' Mr MacKay pointed towards the pitch, 'you are *part of a team.*'

'Yes, sir.' Lee glanced at the clock. Dad would be on the pitch.

Mr MacKay stepped away from the lockers. Plastered flat, his dark hair accentuated his beady eyes and mean mouth.

'*Brooks*,' he snapped, 'the midfield drop back because of *you*.'

'Yes, sir.'

'. . . you're not *reading* the game . . .'

Lee stared at his chewed fingernails, at the mud on his boots. He was letting them down. He'd been letting them down all term. He must *concentrate*.

'We know you can do it, Brooks . . .'

From behind his fringe, Lee caught the pitying glances of his teammates.

'A midfield playmaker creates opportunities: left, right and centre. Am I right?'

'Yes, sir.'

'If I didn't believe you could recover the magnificent form you displayed in the first few months of the season, I'd have replaced you by now.' The frown deepened. 'This half, I want your mind one-hundred-and-ten-per-cent on the game. Can you do it?'

'Yes, sir.'

Mr MacKay's piercing eyes stared long and hard. 'Right!' he said suddenly. 'Good! Now . . . the rest applies to everybody – we're getting the balls, but we're losing them.' He made a fist. '*Maintain* possession. *Push* forward. Keep them on the back foot.' He punched the air. 'Get out there and *GIVE IT TO THEM*!'

197

The team jumped up from the benches and shook their fists. *'Lyndhurst! Lyndhurst! Lyndhurst . . .'* They stomped their boots on the tiles.

Here and there, Lee caught a wink or a nod. As they crowded towards the door, hands patted his back.

'One last thing . . .' Mr MacKay barred the door with his arm. 'The Brooks family have had something of a tough time these last few months, maintaining their privacy from newspapers and TV. The groundsman's on the gate, we shouldn't have trouble with prying eyes, but just in case . . . out there—' Mr MacKay nodded towards the pitch, '– make sure you only use Lee's first name.'

'Lee!' A flash of white – Walton on the wing, pony-tail flapping in the breeze.

Lee looked ahead. One, two, *three* red shirts were closing in for the kill. He cut left, accelerating round them. Defenders fell back.

Stocky Reeves was in the clear just ahead. Price, with his long legs, cruised up easily on the inside.

'Lee!'

He flicked it up and over.

They had them on the run. Time to re-take the middle.

'Take it all the way!' yelled Mr MacKay from the touchline.

Lee pulled in behind Price. Putting on a spurt, Price was heading for the opening.

'Price!' Lee yelled. 'Man on!'

Too late. Price was down.

'Ref!' yelled Mr MacKay. 'Where are your eyes?'

The ref signalled: play on.

Lee took off with the ball, passed to Reeves and moved up.

Reeves chipped it straight back. Nifty.

Reds swooped from all sides. Lee swerved hard right.

'Go on!' screeched Mr MacKay.

Lee cut across the goalmouth. Walton was running in. This was it! Fancy foot-work time. Draw the defence.

'Go on, lad!'

Lee danced. Defenders harried. He zig-zagged. Flipped it. Accelerated round to collect and chipped it straight to Walton's boot.

'YES!'

What a . . . save?! What a keeper! A shot like that!

Lee headed back to his own half.

A pat on the back. 'Nice try!'

Lyndhurst's goalkeeper bounced the ball and studied the field, giving his players a chance to move forward.

Lee ran into position, turned and trotted backwards.

He stopped. There was *that feeling* again – everyone watching him, waiting for him to mess up. He rubbed his neck and looked round.

At the edge of the playing field, over by the fence, something glinted in the sun.

'*Come on, Lyndhurst! Come on, Lyndhurst!*' Mr MacKay led the parents in a chant.

Lee craned his neck. Soaring overhead, the ball dropped deep into the Lyndhurst half.

Red forwards charged.

But Fat Pat got to it, easily. He fed it out to Morris. Morris had buckets of room . . . the reds were on the wrong foot.

Lee put on a spurt – action time again!

Something flashed over by the fence. *Ignore it!* he told himself. Concentrate *one-hundred-and-ten-per-cent!* Don't let Lyndhurst down!

Walton was on the wing and Morris on the inside. Lee took the middle. Reeves was up front, Price and Thorpe slightly behind to the left. A line of whites pushing forward, with Lee in the middle.

'Take it *all the way!*' yelled Mr MacKay.

They crossed the halfway line.

Walton passed inside.

Morris broke formation, veering in sharply towards the centre.

Sunlight flashed again. Suddenly, Lee stumbled, stared and froze; from behind the fence, a long *camera lens* was pointing towards the pitch.

'What are you *playing at?*' roared Mr MacKay.

Lee jerked round. He felt sick; his legs were shaking.

Morris and Price were down. Reeves was surrounded.

Lee clutched his stomach, rubbed his legs and tried to run.

Behind the goal, parents were turning away from the game, towards the car park.

Squinting into the sun, Lee could just make out a group of figures running on to the playing field. They were heading for the pitch . . . their movements were strangely lop-sided . . . they were carrying *cameras!*

'Pass!'

Lee turned back to the game. Blood boomed in his ears; Walton was waving and yelling for all he was worth. Reeves had been tackled. The ball had rolled loose.

Lee sprinted for it . . . misjudged it . . . and went sprawling.

He scrambled to his feet. He still had the ball. Everybody – players on both sides, the parents, the ref – *everybody* was staring at the advancing photographers, as they bobbed and lurched their way towards the goal.

Mr MacKay was pointing and yelling, as if to shoo them away.

'Brooksie! Man on!'

Lee twisted.

Down on one knee, photographers pointed their huge lenses across the pitch.

He twisted again.

Again – photographers raised their cameras, giant eyes homing in on their target.

There was nowhere to run. He took a deep breath. There was nothing else for it . . .

He charged for the touchline. Players from both sides stared as he flew past. With a little skip, he back-heeled the ball just short of touch and kept on going –

right into the group of onlooking parents.

'*Brooksie!*'

'*Lee!*'

'*Brooksie!*'

The photographers, now certain of their target, closed in. Hunters with big guns, they pointed their lenses into the small crowd. The whir, whine and click of cameras began.

THE END

SUDDEN DEATH
Neil Arksey

Flint is hungry for success . . .

When Flint moves out of the children's
home, he gets foster parents and the
longed-for chance to try out for top local
team Wellbeck FC. His foster-father is the
coach. But Aldo, the chairman's son, *hates*
Flint and wants him *out* – especially when
he sees how many goals he can score. And
what Aldo wants, Aldo gets . . .

Flint thirsts for revenge . . .

When a Sudden Death tournament is
announced he decides to fight back. He'll
round up his old mates – other kids written
off as losers in life, just like him – and
they'll *smash* Welbeck.

A gritty, action-packed drama about one
boy who is determined to take all the
chances he can to get ahead in life.

From the author of *Brooksie* and *Flint*.

'Nick Hornby for kids' *Nicky Campbell,
Radio 5 Live*

0 440 864461

A CORGI YEARLING ORIGINAL PAPERBACK

TROUBLEMAKERS
Paul May

Tough enough for the team?

Robbie is desperate to try out for the school football team. He's full of raw talent, skilful and agile, with terrific co-ordination. So why does everybody reckon he's got no chance?

Chester Smith is a top-class professional United player. But his game is falling to pieces, and now he's faced with a continual barrage of ugly taunts from ignorant hooligans in the crowd . . .

Then Robbie and Chester meet, and it could be the beginning of a new chance for each of them. If only they can avoid the troublemakers . . .

An action-packed football tale, *Troublemakers* is hard-hitting, realistic and inspiring.

0 440 86419 4

CORGI YEARLING BOOKS

THE BOTTLE-TOP KING
Jonathan Kebbe

Who said he was a wimp?

Respect. That's what Lewis wants from his classmates. Nicknamed *Useless Lewis* or *Loo Brush*, he's fed up with his stammer, fed up that he can't pluck up the nerve to join the drama club – and fed up that the only football he gets to play is pretend matches with his collection of bottle-tops at home.

Then Lewis's gangly mate Zulfi puts togther a team for a five-a-side charity tournament. And he wants *Lewis* to play! Can the bottle-top king burst out of his timid little shell and show everyone the hero inside?

A fresh, deliciously humorous story of a downtrodden pipsqueak who knows deep down he is a *genius*!

0 440 864674

CORGI YEARLING BOOKS

RIVERSIDE UNITED!
Chris d'Lacey

*When we played Crickle Lane City in the
first round of the Inter-Schools Cup we won
5–1 and I scored a hat trick! Guess what we
had for pudding that day?*

Bread-and-butter pudding. That's Arran
Winters' secret – a big bowl of it the night
before a match. And there's no-one better at
making it than his gran. With her on his
side, Arran – ace superstriker for Riverside
United – *knows* that the Cup belongs to
Riverside!

Then disaster strikes the team, just before
the all-important final. First their midfield
supremo is suspended for fighting. Then
their free-kick specialist gets injured – *and*
their goalie. Arran's suddenly going to need
a whole lot more than a bowl of lucky
pudding if Riverside are to lift the Cup now!

0 440 863996

CORGI YEARLING BOOKS